"SECOND THOUGHTS ALREADY?"

"You'll have to admit . . . this is crazy," Alexandria replied. What had come over her? She'd only met the man this morning and now she was packed and ready for a weekend in God only knew where.

"Craziness, like beauty, is in the eye of the beholder." At the bottom of the steps Sioux stopped. "Alexandria?" he said, his voice low. "Don't change your mind now. Please?"

She turned to face him. "I couldn't if I wanted to, and I don't want to," she admitted with honesty. Grinning impishly she added, "I was never taught to fear hell. Auntie always said she'd hate to enter the Pearly Gates and leave all her friends behind. I guess being crazy is the same way. I don't want to be sent off to the booby-hatch."

"But you don't want to be left behind?" Sioux asked, returning her smile.

Alex answered by opening the front door.

CANDLELIGHT ECSTASY ROMANCES®

TAKE MY HAND

Anna Hudson

A CANDLELIGHT ECSTASY ROMANCE®

Published by
Dell Publishing Co., Inc.
1 Dag Hammarskjold Plaza
New York, New York 10017

Dell ® TM 681510, Dell Publishing Co., Inc.

Candlelight Ecstasy Romance®, 1,203,540, is a registered
trademark of
Dell Publishing Co., Inc., New York, New York.

ISBN: 0-440-18476-2

Printed in the United States of America
First printing—September 1984

Dedicated to Jan Steinkamp
for her cosmetic knowledge and enthusiastic
support,
and to my buddies Frances, Judy, and Norma
at Echo Paperbacks in Irving, Texas,
for hauling me all around doing
research.
You're the best!

To Our Readers:

We have been delighted with your enthusiastic response to Candlelight Ecstasy Romances®, and we thank you for the interest you have shown in this exciting series.

In the upcoming months we will continue to present the distinctive, sensuous love stories you have come to expect only from Ecstasy. We look forward to bringing you many more books from your favorite authors and also the very finest work from new authors of contemporary romantic fiction.

As always, we are striving to present the unique, absorbing love stories that you enjoy most—books that are more than ordinary romance.

Your suggestions and comments are always welcome. Please write to us at the address below.

Sincerely,

The Editors
Candlelight Romances
1 Dag Hammarskjold Plaza
New York, New York 10017

CHAPTER ONE

"Sioux Compton here to see you, Miss Alex."

"Give me a couple of minutes. I need to go over the file." Alexandria Foster, assistant to the president at Lady Jane's Beautiful Cosmetics, opened the manila folder, her caramel-colored eyes quickly scanning the application form and resume.

The soon-to-appear Ms. Sioux, cosmetic chemist, was thirty-four; brown hair, green eyes, and six feet tall. Hmmm, Alex thought as she reviewed the vital statistics. Tall for a woman, but probably statuesque, judging by the weight indicated. Scanning the recommendations, she quickly noted on a pad of paper the applicant's pharmaceutical background.

No problem. Lady Jane preferred training

their employees rather than hiring them away from other cosmetics companies. Hiring women who had extensive experience with another cosmetics firm generally resulted in difficulty orienting them to the Lady Jane philosophy. Her cosmetics empire, from ruler to followers, were women. The cosmetics industry, an industry built for the beautification of women, was controlled by men. Lady Jane's Beautiful Cosmetics was the single exception to the general rule.

Pressing the intercom button, Alex crisply ordered, "Send Sioux Compton in, please."

"Miss Alex, there's something you ought to know," Martha whispered.

Alex interrupted, "Not now, Martha. Later, hon." The soft western drawl, and the casual "hon," kept the order from sounding abrupt.

"But—" came across the communication system.

"Later. Send Ms. Sioux in."

The office door opened immediately and Sioux Compton entered. All six feet of the handsome, impeccably dressed *man* crossed the Persian carpet with long athletic strides toward Alex. Though his name was pronounced the same as the shortened version of Susan, the man drawing closer was the epitome of the wild, dangerous tribe of American Indians.

"Alex?" his deep baritone voice inquired as he

extended his large hand over her solid fruit-wood desk.

"Sioux?" she asked in what she hoped was neither a surprised nor squeaky voice.

"Dad was a Johnny Cash fan," he explained, reminding her of the famous song written about a man who deserted his son, naming him Sue to make him tough enough to face life without a father. "At your service." He eased himself into the cushioned chair directly in front of her. A deep dimple slashed his smoothly shaven left cheek—which had the same effect on Alex as a seductive wink.

Sioux is a man? The upswing of one carefully penciled eyebrow communicated the question.

Her silent question was deflected by the tip of his eyebrow's arrogantly cocking toward his sharply parted dark hair. *Alex is a woman?* The mossy-green eyes shone with an inner sparkle as he appraised her model's figure, long blond hair elegantly twisted into an intricate chignon, defiant amber eyes, and perfect features.

Sioux was not only a man, he was also a full-blooded Indian and, at the moment, feeling extremely primitive. The pounding of blood through his heart could have rivaled the steady beating of a war drum.

Alex, pen still in her left hand, placed a large X over the notes she had taken only moments ago. Men had never been hired at Lady Jane's and never would be. The Equal Opportunity Employment laws could be manipulated by women with an ease equal to that with which their male counterparts managed to ignore them in other companies.

"There seems to be a mistake, Mr. Compton."

"Aren't my papers in order?"

"Well, yes, but the position has been filled."

Alex wasn't about to become involved in a lawsuit filed against the company for reverse discrimination. Five years under Jane's tutelage had given her the ammunition needed to stave off any masculine attack, or in this case, any Indian uprisings.

"The ad is still in the newspaper." Reaching into his breast pocket he extracted a small ad and placed it on the open file beneath her fingertips.

Smiling as though sincerely regretting being the bearer of bad tidings, Alex fingered the torn edges of the ad. "We run this ad for a contracted length of time." Her eyes, frosty, impaled the intruder, daring him to push the issue, as she added, "The position is filled. Now, if you'll excuse me, I have other appointments."

"You hired a woman?" he inquired blandly, not taking the dismissal cue.

"A qualified, competent woman," she lied without blinking so much as an eyelash.

"Probably as feminine as the decor in here," she distinctly heard him murmur.

"This is an office, Mr. Compton, not a bedroom. Lady Jane spent a cool fortune on this decor. What did you expect? Lavender and ruffles?"

Sioux shook his head, lips twisting wryly. "Lavender has a particularly feminine fragrance. This office is exactly what I expected. You are the lavender in this . . . sterile whitewashed cubicle." The soft, seductive note in his voice raked over her skin as silkily as the company's latest moisturizer.

Alex physically recoiled, leaning to the back of her chair, watching his green eyes unclothing her and placing her nude slender body between satin sheets. She'd invited the intimate remark by referring to a private bedroom. But where, she wondered, did this . . . macho male get off criticizing the decor? Typical Macho Max, she thought, stifling an indelicate snort.

"It will be a pleasure working closely with you," he whispered in a low, gravelly tone.

Alex laughed brittlely, tilting forward and propping her elbows on the desk: long, well-manicured fingers steepled, tips pointing toward her straight nose, blocking the smug sweep of her upturned lips. "Amusing," she replied in a condescending tone. "You forgot to

15

include an important item on your resume . . . overconfident."

"Determined would be more appropriate."

"Unemployed . . . and likely to remain that way," she retorted, flipping his folder shut and shoving it toward an isolated corner of the desk.

"Have lunch with me," he demanded rather than requested.

"No, thank you," she refused with the sharpness of a stiletto stabbing through soft wax. Using the cues customary in an interview, she stood, indicating the closing of his interview.

Sioux Compton's narrowed eyes followed the graceful motion appreciatively before he raised himself to his full height. Green eyes, the color of jade, clashed with the hard glint of topaz stone on the same level. He smiled, realizing that Alex Foster was in the fullest sense an exquisite representation of Lady Jane's Beautiful Cosmetics. Her height intrigued his desire to discover, explore the long length of leg he knew was hidden from view.

He had expected automatic rejection. Lady Jane's policy of not hiring men was well known. He had not anticipated being interviewed by a woman who would reject him first as an employee and then as a man. He'd been prepared for one, but not the other. The first he could dismiss with a casual shrug of the shoulders, but the other? That type of rejection was a bitter pill to swallow.

"You won't reconsider?"

"About the job? Or lunch?" she inquired with false sweetness, somewhat relieved she would shortly be out from underneath his microscopic examination. Unbidden, the idea for a masculine fragrance, mossy as his green eyes, a new line for Lady Jane, entered her mind. The soft floral fragrance emanating from the production end of the building jarred against his total maleness, reminding Alex he didn't belong at Beautiful Cosmetics.

"Both."

"Sorry. There is not a job available for a man with your qualifications, and I'm lunching with my secretary."

"I have a formula which could revolutionize the industry," he bargained, trying to entice her into changing her mind.

"You and fifty thousand others," Alex retorted, rejecting the bait. "Sorry, again."

"You probably will be," he attested with a cynical smile that denied her another glance at the appealing dimple. "A man's name suits you . . . *honey,*" he quipped, intending to damage her confidence as effectively as she had whittled on his.

The inference and vocal intonation infuriated Alex. He'd obviously overheard the common western habit she had of calling everyone "hon" or "honey," regardless of gender. *Ignore him,* her business sense told her. With calm precision she stepped from behind her desk, the gentle swaying of her hips denying the implication of her having called another woman "hon."

"Thank you for inquiring about the job. Better luck next time." Graciously she offered her hand as though she were truly unhappy that the position was filled. The warmth of having it encompassed by both of Sioux's palms in an unbusinesslike handshake disturbed Alex, as did the sight of the stark-white cuffs, which contrasted sharply with the tanned, uncommonly smooth masculine hands.

"You could prove me wrong," he murmured quietly, not releasing her tapered fingers.

"The word 'darling' is tossed about from New York to California; in Colorado we use 'hon.' " His sardonic expression goaded her further. *Besides,* she silently fumed, *I proved my femininity for three miserable years . . . nightly. He departed to parts unknown with his secretary, and I was left with the product of my femininity bulging in front of me.* Her spine stiffened as she jerked her hand from between his.

Why was she being so damned defensive? He was the one being rejected, not herself. Ego. He had attacked her ego, her self-concept, the cloak of assuredness she'd adopted years ago. Teeth

18

grinding, she wished she hadn't let him get to her.

"Now, if you'll excuse me, I have to earn a living." Opening her office door, Alex gestured with one arm toward the outer door.

Sioux saw the pain in the depths of her eyes, and then she averted her gaze. He wondered what she'd been thinking. What remembrance had brought that look to her eyes? He hadn't expected any personal revelation from the cool, icy-demeanored woman. He had intended to badger, not to hurt her. Although he instantly regretted having inflicted the pain, her reaction piqued his curiosity. For some reason he was sure the look had something to do with a man. He had reminded her of some painful episode in her past. Who in his right mind could hurt such a beautiful, intelligent woman? A fool, he silently thought as he watched the skin tighten across her high cheekbones and a tinge of pink lightly, naturally, paint her cheeks with a heated flush.

"I'm sorry," he apologized, feeling the words were inadequate. She still refused to face him. He gave her one last penetrating stare, his eyes smoldering in futility. With an inward shrug he followed the path of her eyes and left the office.

"I tried to tell you," Martha said waspishly. "You're always too busy, too rushed, to listen."

The complaint was a common one, and justifiable. Alex raised one hand to stop the tirade

Martha Michaels seemed likely to launch into. Weakly she smiled at her secretary.

"I'm taking a half hour for lunch. You're welcome to join me *if* you treat me with TLC. I only allow one exasperating person in my office a day." Glancing at the outside door, she added pointedly, "The quota for the day just walked out."

Martha grinned. "I wouldn't call him a 'quota'; I'd call him a 'hunk.' Those smoky green eyes were signaling 'Go baby, go!' "

"Your overactive glands are showing," Alex observed with a groan as she leaned against the doorjamb.

"Yeah," Martha answered, batting her eyes and squirming in her seat, "and tonight's the night!"

Tilting her head, Alex sighed dramatically. "Brandon?"

"Ralph," Martha corrected dreamily.

"The Romeo of Wall Street?" Alex scoffed, using the nickname she had given the stockbroker. "He's trouble with a capital T."

"Wrong. Sex with a capital S," Martha responded with a cheeky grin.

Chuckling at her secretary's frankness, Alex gave up trying to stuff some sense into Martha's head. Every woman had to find out the disreputable, lecherous qualities of the male species. It was impossible to convince another woman, regardless of how good a friend she was, that men were a contaminated product which should be quarantined until proven harmless. It was a lesson every woman had to learn for herself, just as she had.

"I'm having lunch with a capital L," Alex said, refusing to be lured into a discussion of her own celibate life-style, which was one of Martha's favorite topics of discussion.

"Do you mind if I take a long lunch hour? I saw this fabulous, slinky—"

"Go! You'll take my lunchtime describing the dress, then leave me stranded while you run over to the shop. Scat!"

Martha hurriedly opened her bottom drawer and grabbed her purse. "I'm gone, boss lady." Quick mincing steps carried her to the door. "The dress would fit you, too, if you wanted to borrow it."

"Out! Out before I change my mind!" Alex shook her fist in mock severity. Martha was a good six inches shorter than herself. Anything she could lend Alex would change a maxilength into a minilength.

Martha winked, reminding Alex of a wink of a different sort, and dashed through the door.

Slowly, Alex turned and reentered her spacious office. The view from the ninth story was spectacular, giving her a feeling of command over the smaller office buildings in downtown

Denver. Being located on the top floor of Lady Jane's Beautiful Cosmetics was indicative of the rise in stature of her own career.

"I should thank Jake the Jerk," she mumbled, heading for the small refrigerator artfully disguised to resemble the storage cabinets which were made of the same cherry wood as the other furniture. A brown bag and soft drink were the solitary occupants of the cool white interior.

Alex pulled them out, shut the door, swiveled her chair around, and sat down. The file folder of Sioux Compton was pushed farther aside, out of her range of vision. She didn't want to think about the man. She dumped the contents, spilling out a peanut-butter-and-jelly sandwich, a large green apple, and a paper napkin. Sinking her sharp front teeth into the apple and breaking a piece off, she munched, dabbing with the napkin at the juice which trickled between her lips.

Slightly annoyed with herself for her overreaction to his obnoxious comments, she made the next bite larger. She hadn't thought about Jake the Jerk, her ex-husband, for ages. At one time Jake the Jerk had been Jake the Giant. He had towered over her five feet nine inches, making her feel small, diminutive, and protected for the first time in her life. His nickname had been an endearment as lavish in praise as the present critical alteration was denigratory of his character.

Jerk was apropos. Who but a jerk would abandon a pregnant woman?

The acidic rind of the apple matched her memories. The fall she had taken on the sidewalk outside this very building had been a disaster, and a relief. The resulting two-week stint in the hospital could have cost her her job, but it didn't. Jane hadn't fired her, but it did cost her the life of her unborn child.

The white tart flesh of the apple reminded Alex of the interview she had had with Jane prior to the accident. Pregnant, scared, but qualified and industrious—those were the qualities Jane had seen. Alex only remembered being pregnant and scared.

Dressed in a deep lilac silk shantung suit, the slender middle-aged, auburn-haired woman had shrewdly placed her wire-framed glasses on her desk when Alex had entered the opulent, white-on-white office. The single color breaking the interior's colorless scheme was the gleam of gold. A large golden horse, unseeing eyes facing the tall windows, was the focal point in the room.

"Alexandria Foster." The long first name twisted and rolled from Jane's beautifully lined lips. "We'll call you Ms. Alex. I don't hire males, but I don't object to short masculine names." A husky chuckle followed the disclosure. "Privileged information, but if you're going to be my right-hand woman, you have to know the ground rules."

"Yes, ma'am," Alex replied respectfully.

"Drop the ma'am. I may be older than you, but I'm a long way from retirement or senility." The bold assessing blue eyes followed the path of Alex's cloth-covered buttons until they reached her waist. "Pregnant?"

"Yes, ma'—Jane. Fourth month." Her chin lifted defiantly. She knew employers' views on hiring a pregnant woman. Polite dismissal after a brief interview was standard operating procedure. Protectively, Alex placed her arm over the unborn child.

"Marriage on the rocks forcing you into the ranks of the unemployed or is it the high cost of living in Denver?"

"Divorce," she answered calmly, her pride tilting her rounded chin up farther.

"Don't want to run home to Mama?"

"No."

Mama couldn't, or wouldn't, welcome a pregnant daughter on her doorstep. A man had destroyed that relationship also. It was hard to have a daughter hanging around the same age as her present husband. No, Alex wouldn't be returning to the nest . . . it was filled.

"Bitter about the divorce?" Jane asked probing past her pride.

"Yes." Her mouth snapped out the single syllable with the steeliness of a well-sprung trap.

"Half the women in Denver are divorced. Don't feel as though you're struggling alone," Jane advised sagely. "I've been there, too. It's why I took a small inheritance and guaranteed my future by building a cosmetics empire." Jane plopped her glasses on her nose and stabbed them back with a pointed index finger. She picked up a gold-toned pen and scribbled a five-figure number on a notepad. "That enough?"

It was more than enough; it was generous beyond reason. Alex could feel her eyes widen in surprise. Unable to speak, she merely nodded her head affirmatively.

Jane chuckled. "Your golden eyes remind me of my trusted steed," she said, grinning and pointing toward the gold horse. "I expect the same from both of you: loyalty and hard work. This isn't a charity house."

"You'll never regret this," Alex had vowed.

Eight years and a firm friendship later, she had unwaveringly kept the promise. In her eyes Jane could do no wrong. People she hired were assessed not only in terms of ability, but of the potentiality for being loyal to the head of the firm. They were all a tight-knit group. All for one and one for all.

The theory men generated that women couldn't work together was disproven daily. The myth that only a male had the business acumen to run a large business was disproven annually in the profit reports. Beautiful Cosmetics was big business, but a simple foundation was the company's formula and motto: Beautiful cosmetics: Beauty made *for* women, *by* women.

Nibbling around the apple core, hunger appeased, Alex tossed the core into the wastebasket. Maybe being riled up at Sioux Compton had served a purpose. She needed occasionally to recollect where she had come from and what she had become. At twenty-nine she had come a long way from being the insecure woman she had been. The bitterness had faded. She was too busy to dwell on what had taken place in the past.

Deciding not to eat the sandwich, she put it back in the brown sack and tucked it into the refrigerator for another day. Stretching, she walked to the window and looked out.

"Alex!" Martha burst into the office without knocking. "Oh, you've already spotted the trouble we're in." Directing Alex's vision to the street below the window, she watched for the explosive reaction.

"So?" Alex inquired.

She saw a lone man with a large sign walking back and forth in front of Beautiful Cosmetics.

Occasionally he would wave to a car that must have been honking.

"That's your Ms. Sioux down there practicing his war dance. Wait till you see what it says!"

CHAPTER TWO

Alex grimaced, pivoting away from the window. "I guess it's time for someone to rain on his parade."

"You going to pour water on him?" Martha asked with an impish grin.

"Not a bad idea. He has all the instincts of a dog in the front yard," Alex gritted, striding toward the door. "You notify Jane; I'll take care of the rebellion."

Hands on her hips, Alex waited until Sioux had finished walking away from her toward the end of the block and had turned around. She wasn't about to make herself look ridiculous by trotting along after him.

Lady Jane un-American.
Refuses to hire Sioux.

Alex could feel her eyes bugging out of their sockets as she read the huge placard.

"Of all the unmitigated nerve," she ground out between clenched teeth. Storming in his direction, she no longer cared about appearances, or the blasts of horns from the busy street. Alex had the urge to use a few of the brutal forms of deadly torture the tribe he hailed from had used against early settlers. Scalping was too good for him. She wanted him spread-eagle, tied to stakes on the hot sidewalk, and fried like a raw egg.

"Do you want to be sued for slander?" she demanded when within shouting distance.

Shooting her his warmest, most disarming smile, he propped the pole on which the sign was mounted against one hip and waited for her to get closer. According to his prearranged strategy, getting the hiring agent out of the office building into the public eye had been essential. As he watched tendrils of silvery-blond hair being blown loose from the pins holding it, he wished momentarily that Alex weren't going to be the victim of his sneak attack.

"Do you spell sue, S-I-O-U-X?" he asked with a teasing glint in his bright eyes. "Sioux for slander? How about S-U-E for sexual discrimination against a member of a minority group?" Lazily he closed the small gap between them.

"You're crazy, do you know that? You can't S-U-E anybody. The vacancy is filled!"

"Let's have a powwow over lunch and smoke a peace pipe," he suggested, edging even closer.

"Stop the Indian jargon. You're no more an Indian than I'm a Denver Cowgirl," she huffed.

They were beginning to draw the attention of the pedestrians walking down the street. A strand of hair blew into her mascara-coated eyelashes, clinging to their curling sootiness. She saw Sioux's hand moving toward her temple and angrily slapped at it. The last thing she wanted was to have this . . . wild man touching her in plain view of the people who were beginning to make a half-moon circle around them.

"She refuses to hire me, refuses to eat with me, and refuses to listen to me," he complained to the growing crowd. "What do you think I can do to prove I'm not on the warpath?" he asked one senior citizen who was leaning on her knotted-pine cane, avidly watching.

"Well, sonny, in my day a real man would have swung the reticent lady up in those brawny-looking arms of yours, and carried her away."

It was obvious to Sioux that the elderly lady thought this was some sort of publicity stunt and was thoroughly enjoying it.

"You lay one finger on me and I'll whack you

with your own billboard," Alex threatened quietly near his ear.

"Naw," an aging man disagreed. "Kiss 'er here where we can all see. Then carry her off into the sunset."

Alex could see the mischievous twinkle in the green eyes glowing brightly slightly above her own. She had to stop this insanity. She'd read about crowds gathering in New York City to witness a sexual assault, but she'd never heard of the crowd inciting the assault.

"He's a mad scientist," Alex condemned. "Crazy as a loon."

"Crazy in love, it looks like, lady," came from the back of the group.

"Kiss 'er," the old man encouraged, nudging Sioux closer to Alex.

A chant began as the same man turned to his fellow spectators and began directing them as though they were a church choir.

"Kiss 'er! Kiss 'er! Kiss 'er!"

Sioux snaked his arm around Alex's slender waist as she started to turn and run. "You wouldn't want to disappoint the public, Beautiful Cosmetics's potential customers, would you?"

"Yes," Alex hissed, leaning back, keeping her torso away from his chest.

Sioux laughed, his head tossed back. This whole episode was going better than he had planned. The *mob* crowd was becoming larger and larger with each passing moment. Cars were no longer zooming past; they were slowing down as the rubberneckers craned out their windows to see what was going on. The chant became louder and louder as more voices began shouting the two words.

He saw his friend approaching, camera in hand. "It will be worth it in the long run," he whispered huskily into her ear.

Alex had never been so flustered in her life. A man she had met less than thirty minutes ago was about to kiss her, in broad daylight, right next to one of the busiest streets in Denver, and there was nothing she could do about it. Squirming against the cradle of his hips had not gained her release. She wanted to pound, scratch out her frustration on his face, shoulders, and chest, but couldn't picture herself behaving in such an unladylike, violent manner.

"Want to see how long that gorgeous hair of hers is?" Sioux asked the crowd.

A roar of yeses interspersed the deafening demand to "Kiss 'er!"

"Let go of me, you heathen," Alex demanded, placing the spike of her high-heeled shoe squarely on the end of his wing-tip shoe. Her toe moved in an arc as she ground her heel down.

The smile on Sioux's face broadened. He didn't wince. He didn't move his foot. The stoicism of generations kept any trace of pain from showing on his face. He wedged the long pole of the placard between the outside of his shoe and the crook of his arm, and lazily began removing the hairpins which kept her hair in place. Each one hit the concrete pavement making a light tinny sound. His green eyes blazed into hers when she put more weight into the grinding of her stiletto heel.

When the last pin fell to the ground, the uncommonly soft hand of her adversary raked through her waist-length hair, spilling it over the arm clamped around her waist. Alex could no longer hear the chant for the blood pounding in her ears. She no longer noticed the fifty or so people circling around them; her golden eyes had been mesmerized by the emerald fires above her. She'd stopped grinding her heel when she realized that inflicting pain would not gain her freedom.

Fatalistically she waited for the kiss the strangers were demanding. It would come. There was no doubt in her mind that Sioux Compton had every intention of avenging the damage done to his toe by applying an equal amount of pressure to her mouth. She only hoped the mixture of fear and anticipation couldn't be read in her eyes.

With the greatest of patience Sioux seductively took her lips. He had felt, on her writhing against him during her attempt to flee, the tightening below his waist, and had been able to control the awakening involuntary reaction. His plan did not include being embarrassed when their bodies separated. Although he had mentally blocked any feeling of pain from the rotating pressure of her heel, he was finding the softness of her breasts pressed against him, the silky feel of her hair wrapped around him by the wind, the sweet texture of her lips, testing the power of his will.

Her eyes open, she fought the impulse to wrap her arms around his broad shoulders and lean into his masculine strength. The repeated flash of daytime lightning was her undoing. The sound of hands clapping matched the flurrying of wings inside her stomach that spread to lower points with tingling arousal. Encouraging cheers and war whoops carried her deeper into his awaiting arms. The taste and feel, the sounds and sights, all blended together in an erotic mixture she couldn't deny. Nothing in her past, not even the marriage bed, had had the same impact.

"Alexia." She heard the stranger groan a name other than her own, breaking the spell he'd spun.

My God! I'm being seduced by a man who doesn't know my name!

"Alexandria!" she corrected, flinging herself away from the warm prison his arms had made.

"Alex . . . what's going on?" This new voice belonged to Lady Jane, her boss.

The heat that had been captured in the cavity of her chest flooded upward in an explosive, fiery red, staining her neck and face as it crept to her hairline. It was bad enough having strangers and sightseers witness her willing surrender into the stranger's arms, but to have the woman she'd admired, modeled herself after, see her in Sioux's clutches was too much.

"I've got it!" a grinning, lanky spectator shouted as he waved his camera. "Thanks, Sioux!"

Immobilized by the rapid turn of events, Alex stood, Sioux's arm draped across her shoulders, watching the face of her boss as the crowd began to disperse.

"I repeat. What's going on?" Jane inquired, her eyes skipping from Alexandria's beet-red face to the huge placard.

"How do you do? My name's Sioux. You must be Lady Jane?" Alex heard her nemesis introducing himself while she remained stunned, tongue tied, unable to do anything other than gulp air into her lungs.

"Newspaperman?" Jane asked, pointing to the lanky man running down the street, stopping beside an old Jeep and climbing in hurriedly.

Sioux nodded affirmatively. The attack against Beautiful Cosmetics, carefully planned and staged, had been executed efficiently, effectively, but his conscience revolted against the necessary involvement of Alexandria. The pain he had seen earlier was minuscule when compared to the agony on her face now.

"You lousy . . ." Alex began, but was stilled by the firm hand of Lady Jane calmly placed on her forearm, moving her away from Sioux.

"We can expect to be seen on the front page of *The Rocky Mountain News* tomorrow. Right?" Jane inquired.

"If it's a particularly good shot they might hold it for the Sunday edition," he replied smoothly. "You know, human interest, that sort of thing."

Alex mentally visualized the picture and the caption and groaned aloud. Fires of hate flicked over the rawness of her exposed emotions. The eyes which had mesmerized her earlier held a look of . . . what? Pity? Sorrow? Victory! With the quiet steps of his ancestors he had sneakily overwhelmed her. She had been Colorado's equivalent of a Benedict Arnold. Bile rose in her throat as her stomach churned with the rapidity of one of the blenders in a large vat in the manufacturing section of the building complex.

"You lousy sonofa—" The squeezing pressure on her arm halted the completion of the imprecation.

"May I suggest we continue this discussion in privacy?" Lady Jane suggested with icy calmness.

"Certainly. Lead the way," Sioux agreed amiably. Straws stuck beneath his fingernails would have hurt less than the hatred he was getting from Alex. His strong, goal-oriented motivation, his determination to be hired, was weak armament against the barbed rake of her golden eyes across his immobile face.

They filed into the building Indian style, Lady Jane, Alex, then Sioux.

Alex berated herself with each and every step she took. The smiles on the faces of the women she passed went by unnoticed. She walked behind her mentor and in front of her tormentor with crisp steps which belied her inner turmoil. There was no way to warn Jane of what had taken place in her office without that damned wild-man overhearing her.

Irrationally, she couldn't help but wish time could be turned back a hundred years and Sioux could be confined to a reservation which contained the most dangerous of Indian rebels. He wouldn't have been able to plague her orderly life, threaten the stability of her employment, or wreak havoc on her equilibrium. Alex's inner rage was outside the boundaries of clear thinking. She wanted revenge in the worst way. Sioux Compton had won this skirmish, but, by God, he wasn't going to conquer her territory, she vowed.

Lady Jane pointed toward the two icy-blue couches which faced each other over a low glass-topped coffee table near the floor-to-ceiling windows in Alex's office.

"Alex, would you please get Mr. Sioux's file?" she requested, her accent elongating each syllable.

She's madder than a wet hen protecting her brood, Alex realized. The only time her Missouri accent became obvious was when she was keeping tight rein on her temper.

"The last name is Compton, Lady Jane," Sioux informed her quietly.

"Mr. Compton, would you be so kind as to explain what has taken place? What do you want from Beautiful Cosmetics?"

Sioux recapped the interview, leaving out the personal volleys between himself and Alexandria, pausing only long enough to rise slightly from his seat when Alexandria placed herself on the sofa beside her boss.

He ended by saying, "It's simple. I want to work for Lady Jane's Beautiful Cosmetics."

"Mr. Compton, I'm a woman, but don't insult my intelligence by trying to make me believe the sign you were carrying wasn't professionally made, nor that the timely arrival of the press was unplanned. You planned this attack down to the last detail." Lady Jane—the honorary title would have been Four-Star General had she been born a male. She was a master strategist. She had to be to have so quickly seen through the underlying details of his master plan.

"Guilty as charged," Sioux confessed with a boyish grin. "Your policy, your motto, is well known in the pharmaceutical industry."

Jane removed his file from Alex's lap and cast her a reassuring smile. Alex could almost hear her saying, "We aren't beaten until we wave the white flag." As Lady Jane flicked through the application form and the stack of letters of recommendations, Alex knew she was planning a delaying tactic, or possibly would find a weakness in his forces.

"No cosmetics background," Jane murmured aloud.

"Others in your organization have risen to the top without *any* formal training, or experience," he replied, pointedly glancing from Jane to Alexandria.

The unspoken accusation that Alexandria was a prime example of the fact, pointing again to her being the weak link in the strong golden chain of her defenses, rankled against Alex's already ragged nerves.

"I've earned every promotion I've received," Alex huffed defensively.

"Ahhhh, I'm certain you speak the truth, but with a forked tongue. You were *hired* because you're a woman and promoted for your diligent loyalty to Lady Jane, not because you were qualified originally for the position." Sioux leaned forward, forearms casually propped against his muscular thighs. "I'm qualified for the position of head chemist, and I have a product which should make Beautiful Cosmetics a billion-dollar industry."

"What age-old, magical potion has the medicine man passed on to you?" Alex asked, disparaging his claim.

Sioux chuckled, undaunted by her sarcasm. "Ms. Alex, I'd be a crazy Indian for certain if I divulged the formula. When I have a contract, signed and sealed by"—his tanned finger pointed toward Jane—"the Great White Mother, I'll be more than happy to cooperate. If we can come to some agreement by midnight, I might also be able to stop that photo from appearing in *The Rocky Mountain News,*" he added.

"You know the white man broke every treaty signed with the Indians, don't you?" Jane asked, probing, seeking a weakness in his spearheaded attack.

"This is the twentieth century, not the nineteenth. We've learned how to negotiate precise terms. In 1924 we even managed to get voting privileges . . . I might add, shortly after women's suffrage."

Alex's hostility was defused by Jane's soft chuckles. Had he managed to disarm Jane? Did she see he was manipulating her with his smooth talk of an imaginary wonder potion which was probably as phony as his ridiculous name?

"So you really are an Indian?" Alex asked, wanting to damage his credibility.

"Pure bred," Sioux replied, spearing her with green fire. He'd been the recipient of prejudiced remarks and inquiries and had grown callous. Perhaps his Johnny Cash explanation of his name was a telltale defense mechanism he'd used since childhood, but he didn't think so. He was proud of his heritage. As proud of who he was and of having pulled himself up by his bootstraps as any blue-blooded immigrant whose ancestors had arrived on the *Mayflower*.

"Would you object to Alex and me having a private counsel?" Jane asked, smiling in Sioux's direction.

"Not at all. Shall I wait in the outer office or down on the sidewalk?" Sioux teased, almost smelling victory.

"Please, the outer office. Unless, of course, you have television cameras waiting for your appearance," Jane responded jokingly.

Sioux laughed, shook his head negatively, and with the grace of a Texas bobcat rose and strode toward the door. A quick glance over his shoulder reminded him of the wooden masks carved to keep the demons and wicked spirits away. Both women were scowling. Lady Jane had given the false appearance of a smiling General Custer. His own smile sagged as he quietly closed the door behind him.

Jane quickly stood and moved to the windows. Alex was completely taken off balance when her boss swung back around and asked, "Are you prejudiced?"

"No!" she replied, shocked by the question.

"Damned good thing. I'd fire you and hire him to replace you if you were. Part of my own private war has been fueled by the prejudice against women. There's no way in hell I'll tolerate it from an employee! Your sharp tongue needs to be curbed around that young man."

"But—"

"But nothing. Prejudice has its roots firmly based in stupidity. I refuse to associate with, or employ, ignorant, biased personnel."

"Can you deny a prejudice against men? Isn't that what Beautiful Cosmetics, made for women, by women, is all about?" Alex argued.

"No, ma'am," Jane drawled. "Beautiful Cosmetics is a last-ditch effort to employ women, offering them opportunities they are denied in

42

the corporate structure of other companies. A man can go anywhere and get a job; a woman has to scrounge and search, and is usually prohibited from using the God-given potential she has. The cornerstone of my company is not based on the sandy foundation of prejudice; it's based on preservation of the female work ethic."

"But I thought . . . you instructed me . . ." Completely baffled by the direction of the conversation, Alex couldn't string a coherent thought together.

Jane walked over and patted Alex on the arm affectionately. "I *encouraged* the misconception, and will take the responsibility for your attitude. When I hired you I knew you were angry with the male species." Jane shrugged; a rose tint which matched her tailored suit spread from beneath her white ruffled blouse up to her jawline. "It's time to climb off my soapbox and level with you. We're in trouble if the Office of Economic Opportunity gets wind of our refusing to hire a member of a minority group. They've looked the other way on our all-women hiring policy, but they won't ignore a claim of ethnic discrimination."

"Can't we use the same ploy we've always used—we hired a woman who was better qualified?" Alex inquired as she rose to her feet and walked to the filing cabinet. "There have been other applicants."

"Equally qualified?"

Alex shook her head. "Not so far, but I have appointments scheduled throughout the remainder of the week. Surely we can find a woman who has better qualifications."

"Delaying tactic. That's what we need. How are we going to keep Chief Green Eyes off the employee roster?" Jane asked, rubbing from one corner to the other the tip of her pink fingernail.

"Can we make our hiring him contingent upon this miracle product he has supposedly created?" Alex suggested, searching for the weak link in his resume.

"Maybe. He perceives you, mistakenly, as I did, as prejudiced against him for his Indian blood, and for being a male. We can use that." Jane crossed one arm against her chest; the other bent upward, her fingers strumming the side of her face thoughtfully. "Right now the situation is volatile. We have to lead him into a blind canyon, then bar him inside . . . or, in this case, *outside* the walls of Beautiful Cosmetics."

"I've managed to botch this from start to finish. I can't believe he kissed me in broad daylight and—"

"That's it! Being hired by an all-female firm is

44

his first priority, but what's his second priority? I watched him. He's attracted to you." Jane's sharp blue eyes narrowed, sweeping over Alex from head to foot. "What if you were the bait inside the blind canyon?" she hypothesized. "He thinks you've rejected him for all the wrong reasons. His premise is faulty."

"You want *me* to . . ." Alex's blind loyalty to Jane, her mentor, her friend, her confidante, was being tested.

Jane draped her arm across Alex's shoulders and hugged her in a motherly fashion. "I want you to give the appearance of meeting his demands. No contracts. No commitments. Perhaps you can even persuade him to call off the dogs at the newspaper office. Just keep him diverted until we can find a woman who outshines him in any court of law."

Alex swallowed, gulping air into her nervous stomach. "Jane, I'd do anything for you, but I honestly don't think I can carry this off. The man makes me want to scream and yell obscene abuses."

Laughing sincerely for the first time, Jane moved toward the door. "You can do anything you make up your mind to do. Isn't that the reason for the growth in sales figures? We train our women to be confident in their own abilities. Our friendly competitor, Mary Kay Cosmetics, illustrates that with the bumblebee.

45

Aerodynamically it can't fly, but it defies man's theories on the laws of flight and merrily buzzes from flower to flower. Think positively, Alex. Let our 'brave' man hear the hum of your wings, admire the way you defy the elements . . . then sting him. Ready?" she asked, poised at the door, hand on the knob.

Alex nodded her head. Pasting a plastic smile on her face, she watched Jane slowly open the door, reaching out to beckon the return of Sioux Compton. Loyalty, fidelity, and friendship, not to mention employment, were high stakes in the game she was about to begin. The single thought which kept the smile on her face when he entered the door was: *He unscrupulously used me. Turnabout is fair play.*

CHAPTER THREE

"We've decided to consider you for the position of head chemist. Alex will show you around the plant; make you familiar with our product and our philosophy," Jane offered regally, as though she were giving him an opportunity to be admitted into her realm.

"Great!" Sioux enthused. "Would you mind my making a phone call first?"

"Be my guest," Alex said, removing the phone from its cradle and punching the number nine for an outside line. "Shall we leave?"

"Would you mind?" Sioux asked. He was quizzically tilting his head at her shift in gears from open hostility to gracious hospitality.

"Of course not," she replied, smiling insincerely. *The nerve of the man. Well, Mr. Sioux, watch out for snipers!*

The title Lady well suited the older woman as she regally swished from the room, her first lady-in-waiting close on her heels. Sioux watched their exit with a slight quirk lifting the corner of his mouth. There was a mixture of pride and pain in his temporary victory. Pride in having successfully accomplished the feat of being at least temporarily accepted; pain at having manipulated Alexandria. He no longer thought of her as Alex. The masculine name was incongruous with the entirely feminine curves he had felt pressed against him while Bill was busily snapping pictures for *The Rocky Mountain News*.

"Billy Hayman, please," Sioux requested from the switchboard operator at the paper.

"Yeah?" he heard his friend respond a few seconds later.

"Put a wrap on those pictures. The lid on Beautiful Cosmetics wasn't as tough to open as we thought it would be," Sioux said, chuckling at Billy's intake of breath.

"Too late. The editor thinks this is a great human interest story. You know: reverse discrimination. The poor-male-downtrodden-by-the-Wicked-Black-Widow scenario. I'll try to have them hold back on it as long as I can, but I'd have to throw my skinny body between the wheels of the presses to stop this from being in print by Sunday."

An untypical expletive was Sioux's singular retort as he slammed the receiver down. He hadn't planned on Lady Jane's capitulating. He had expected to have to force her hand with public notoriety. Strumming his fingertips on the polished fruitwood finish of the desk, he worried about the effect this "human interest" article would have on the two women. Would public pressure infuriate Lady Jane and Alex? They'd both been purring when they left the office. How would they react to being the subject of an exposé? Sioux plowed his fingers through his hair, then rose to his feet and with a loose gait strode to the door. The frontal-attack strategy he had planned was going awry. The only way to kill the story was to make it invalid. Between now and midnight he had to press his advantage to the hilt. One way or another he had to have a commitment from Alexandria.

His fingers circled the knob on his side of the door. Perhaps the chemical elements drawing him to Alexandria were mutual. Sioux snorted. He'd heard of women sleeping their way to the top, but he found the idea repugnant. Should he risk entrusting her with the product which had inspired him to leave his former position? Should he tell her why Beautiful Cosmetics had been chosen as the company to represent the product? Sioux was in a quandary of his own making. *Damn Billy and his camera!*

Alexandria and Lady Jane were seated, heads close together, whispering fervently back and forth when he quietly opened the door. It was evident that the president of Beautiful Cosmetics was pressuring her right-hand woman into something they both found distasteful. Victory isn't that close at hand, Sioux quickly surmised as he watched Alexandria vehemently shaking her head.

"Alexandria!" Martha exclaimed when she glanced to the inner office door and saw the scowling features of Sioux Compton.

Both women jumped as though they had been shot for exchanging secret information. The pained expression Sioux had seen on Alexandria's face flickered toward him for an instant before she schooled her features into a smooth, composed demeanor.

"I'm ready when you are," Sioux said amiably, hiding his own indecisive state with a broad smile which deepened the seductive dimple in his cheek.

"What would you like to see first?" Alex asked while fluidly rising to her feet.

Three buttons undone below that stark white bow, his libido answered silently. "Anything of mutual interest," he replied, governing his tongue to a suitable reply.

Their eyes, caramel coating green as though she were the sweet candy covering a tart green apple at Hallowe'en, conveyed a message that Sioux, the man, couldn't ignore.

The light came on with the force of an icy winter storm. She's been instructed to use her feminine powers on me, Sioux conjectured. Automatically his hand rose to the protective symbol hanging from golden links that circled his neck. His smile showed both rows of even white teeth against his dark complexion as he realized he was going to be the willing participant in a mutual seduction. He wondered just how far Alexandria's loyalty would allow her to go. As far as the bedroom, he hoped. He felt his masculinity rising to the occasion.

"I'll get back to the matter we were discussing," Lady Jane said, breaking their eye contact, speaking first to Alex, then to Sioux. "You should find the production plant interesting, Sioux."

"Undoubtedly," he responded wickedly. Mentally he pictured Alexandria pressing him into dark corners, stroking, petting . . . "Undoubtedly."

Minutes later a combination of floral bouquets assaulted Sioux's nose as they neared the production room. The silence between the two of them was fraught with sexual tension. Alex peeped slightly upward as they walked down the empty corridor. The peptalk Jane had given her had recalled her uninhibited response to this tall, dark stranger who threatened to invade more than the private domain of Beautiful Cosmetics. She wondered if his expertise in kissing could be duplicated. The pink tip of her tongue flicked over her bottom lip.

Nearing the double swinging doors, she reached into her jacket pocket for the small cap which federal law required all employees to wear when working. Drat the man for pitching my hairpins into the wind, she fulminated.

"You'll have to wear one," she instructed, reaching into a packet immediately outside the doors. "Too bad your friendly cameraman isn't here now." A husky laugh took the sting from her words: he had ludicrously covered his head, hairline to hairline, with the white cap.

"How are you going to get this"—his hands lifted a long length of hair—"into one?" He studied the silky, multicolored shades of blond hair as though analyzing each individual strand for color and texture.

Saucily, seeing his intent interest, Alex asked, "Have you perfected a bleach which matches nature's coloring?"

Sioux brought the lock closer to his eyes, wrapping the length around his knuckles, drawing her closer. "Impossible."

His thumb rubbed against the sheen highlighted by the bright overhead lights. When Alexandria raised her arms, lifting the ridiculous cap so that it covered only the top part of his dark hair, her hands fluttering over the shorter hair at his temples, her closeness was almost his undoing. The light touch, the lighter fragrance surrounding her, her uptilted smiling face, made him want to crush her softness against him. She was tempting. . . .

"Only the top hairs fall out," she informed him, her throat tightening over the benign words.

Deliberately she ran her fingers down the length of his lapel. Hadn't Jane told her to disarm him? Make him think that not only Beautiful Cosmetics was falling at his feet, but herself as well? Why was the directive mentally distasteful, but emotionally appealing? The light-brown flecks in his eyes glinted, intensifying the brilliance of the brighter green.

"Then, you won't have to cover yours." He sighed softly. His hand unwound her hair as he mentally veered off from the direction his errant thoughts were taking him. Their closeness was debilitating, especially as he had accidentally brushed the soft curve of her breast against the back of his hand while hastily extracting his fingers.

She's not interested in Sioux Compton, he reminded himself. She's playing Mata Hari for her boss. His eyes became slits as they honed in on the innocence in her eyes. *She is cold-bloodedly seducing me,* he thought, dredging up a barrier to place mentally between the temptation of her parted lips, which were beckoning him with their sweet invitation. His unfettered hand raked against the charm around his neck again. Searching for a protective device to ward off her appeal, he reminded himself of who had given him the charm. His mother, an Indian, a woman whom Alexandria would probably scorn should they be personally introduced. A small flame of outrage ignited within him.

Stepping firmly backward, he asked politely, "Shall we?"

"Shall we what?" Alex asked, bemused, disoriented by his abrupt withdrawal. She'd forgotten about her assigned mission and had been lost in the physical chemistry, which had drawn her closer and closer.

"Get on with the tour," he replied curtly.

Alex winced as though slapped back to reality. *Whatever explosions are taking place, they're one sided*, she reflected derisively. The man underneath the ridiculous white cap rakishly straightened it as though it were a feathered warbonnet.

"We can't let anything get in the way of our common goal, can we?" Sioux murmured sardonically.

He wasn't about to allow a bigot to seduce him. He could sell his product to any number of cosmetics companies who would pay him a small fortune and hire him in a snap. He didn't have to negotiate terms with this oh-so-alluring woman. Inwardly sighing, he knew he did. He'd made a vow and his honor demanded he keep it. Aside from his promise, he also remembered he had to have a decision made by midnight to stop the presses. If Alexandria wanted to play the role of seductress, perhaps he would be wise to follow her lead.

With a quick twist of her hair Alex plopped it on top of her head and rammed on the cap. *Damn it, Jane, you ask too much from me! How am I going to manipulate this man when I can't even control the reactions of my own body?* Straightening her shoulders, mentally shoving an icicle down her spine, she pushed against the swinging door.

"This is the quarantine room. Products purchased from other manufacturers are isolated until the chemist tests them for purity," she informed him in her I'm-the-guide, you're-the-tourist voice.

"Don't insult my intelligence. I'm no novice," he warned, prickling at the casual dismissal in her attitude.

Braggart, she silently denounced. "Fine," she concurred verbally, angrily striding between the barrels toward the production-line room. Her progress was swiftly curtailed by his hand gently restraining her momentum.

55

"There are times, Miss Alex, when I could cheerfully throttle you with my bare hands," he ground out between his tightly clenched jaws.

"Oh?" she asked with sweet perversity. "I thought your specialty was skinning your victims, inch by inch." *It certainly hasn't taken him any time at all to get underneath my tough hide,* she admitted to herself, choking on the tidbit of information.

"We've refined our technique. Now we specialize in seduction of the enemy, regardless of how personally distasteful we find the chore."

"Forewarning me?" Alex hissed, the palm of her hand itching to wipe the feral curl from his sensuous mouth.

"We always let out a war whoop before we attack," he snarled. "We aren't unscrupulous enough to sneak around or hide our contempt behind sticky sweetness."

"Hypocrisy? That item wasn't listed on your resume, either. Sneaking into my office . . . using a woman's name to get past the guard . . . isn't that hypocritical? Having a sign hidden in the bushes isn't an ambush strategy? Didn't I recognize the chant of 'Kiss 'er' as a war whoop? You and your refined technique are despicable!"

"It will all be worth it," he retorted dispassionately, reminding himself of his ultimate goal. "The end will justify the means."

He dropped her arm at the same moment she

56

jerked away. Alex glared at the fierce expression on his face. How could he stoically stand there spouting philosophy when her blood was boiling? Why hadn't her tongue-lashing provoked some reaction? Her arm arched toward his jaw with a mind of its own, physically lashing out at his serene composure. The sound of the slap resounded in the high-ceilinged warehouse. Sparks of pain shot from her stinging palm, up her wrist, to her shoulder, then to her palpitating heart.

"Oh, my God," she whispered, staring at her hand as though it were an alien appendage. "I'm sorry." She was sincerely apologetic.

Sioux felt the fire in his face as though her hand had branded him. The frozen expression continued to hide the raging fire of retaliation which threatened to erupt. *I don't strike women,* he mentally gritted to himself, *regardless of what they do.*

"White women can't control themselves, can they?" he icily observed. Head bent, he tugged with his thumb and forefinger at the white cuff beneath his suit jacket. He knew his mild countenance and verbal jab would be more effective in their open hostility than would physical abuse.

"I said I was sorry!" she argued, unable to deny her intent of blocking his goal of being hired by Beautiful Cosmetics.

57

"You're probably sorrier about the sexual time-bomb ticking away between us. You won't admit it, but you hunger for what you consider to be off limits."

Alex swallowed her self-righteous indignation over his refusal to accept her apology. She couldn't ignore the truth. He had infiltrated past the reserve she maintained while around the opposite sex.

Men, all men, were off limits . . . forbidden. The agony she had suffered during her brief marriage had left her heart scarred. Sioux had managed to slice through the tough façade which she had carefully guarded and which had kept her from responding to another man. Her head dropped in resignation.

"I can't deny the attraction," she confessed solemnly as though admitting the truth would vindicate the atrocity of having struck him.

"Don't expect me to applaud your honesty at this point," he remarked, his head lowering for the first time since she had struck him.

Her bowed head, the body language of a person who was suffering defeat, sent a wash of protective instincts through his body. She had slapped him, cut him to the quick with her sarcastic barbs, but he inexplicably wanted to raise her head and kiss away the hurt and pain from her eyes. He was treading on thin ice, and knew it.

Masochists relish self-inflicted pain; temperate men avoid it. With the advantage of hindsight he was fully aware of her potential to hurt him in a way he had never allowed. The wounds she had knowingly inflicted on his pride, his own hidden wounds, were internally bleeding. She had the power to manipulate and destroy the finer instincts which made him want to salve their mutual wounds. In anger he had wanted to purge his body of its suffering by plunging his manliness into her softness, by making his physical dominance indisputable. Sioux shuddered. He was a healer, not a defiler, of women.

"I can't deny it, either," he uttered hoarsely. "God, I wish I could."

The desire to heal rather than hurt won out as he curved his finger and lightly placed it under her chin, slowly raising it the fraction of an inch needed to put their eyes on the same level. He'd kissed her once in jest; he kissed her now with barely restrained passion. The sealed soft lips clung to him, parting, opening, welcoming the intimacy of his tongue.

Sioux had known she would taste sweeter than raw honey, but he hadn't expected his taste buds to explode, his tongue to become rigid as he dipped into each hidden crevice. Green eyes closed, nostrils flaring, inhaling her scent, he let his imagination carry them out of the bounds of the silent warehouse into a field of blooming wildflowers. In his mind's eye he could see her arms twining them together as he felt his shoulders being hesitantly, then more boldly, stroked. He could feel the tips of her breasts puckering, hardening, as they pressed into the muscles beneath his shirt. Mentally he knew he should withdraw from the intoxicating effects of Alexandria, but he couldn't.

A muffled groan came from the back of his throat as he cupped the soft roundness below her spine, raised her on tiptoe, and brushed his fiery loins against the heat radiating from the juncture of her thighs. Once, twice, three times, he gently squeezed, communicating his need. Moistly her lips responded in the same rhythm as she sipped his marauding tongue. With the pointed tip of his tongue he parodied the fantasy in his mind. He filled her mouth as he imagined stretching, filling her tightness with his manhood. She was hot, moist, pulling him closer, deeper. Her enticing body pressed against him in an upright position as it did in the horizontal picture of his imagination.

He wanted to feel the sleek satin texture of her skin. In his dream, and in reality, he freed one hand to unbutton her clothing, and at the same instant felt a slight tug on the sparse mat of hair on his chest as her fingers wiggled beneath his third and fourth button. Inwardly he groaned in frustration. His imagination running rampant was far faster, far surer, than the reality of making love while upright.

"Alexandria . . . Alexandria," he whispered fervently, breaking contact with her lips. "You're driving me wild, woman. It isn't humanly possible to love you . . . here." The urgency of his need made his voice harsh as he strung wet kisses down her long, slender neck. "It's as though sometime in another life we were lovers. I know the feel of you. The dusty pink color of your breasts. I need to taste them again . . . to savor them. I need to feel your hands wrapped around me, guiding me, leading me to heaven. Forget everything," he pleaded, "come with me. Let me love you; let me love you." His pelvis ground through her light summer suit, explicitly inviting her body to join his. "We'll make wild, savage love, again and again, until you've forgotten who or what I am."

From the instant Sioux had penetrated her lips, Alexandria had mutely committed herself to the pleasures she had for so long forsworn. She had been married, had enjoyed the loving expression of a man and woman. She couldn't turn a deaf ear to his desire, to her own flaming, dewy response.

Any thought of Jane's instructions was forgotten. The woman, not the cosmetics executive, wanted Sioux. By entering the closed circle she had emotionally drawn around herself, by blasting past her sharp tongue, by melting the hard wax at the core of her heart, he had driven her professional image to the far background.

"Yes, Sioux," she softly whispered next to the lobe of his ear, and took a nibble at his skin. Her tongue rolled the flesh against her sharp teeth. "It's been so long, so terribly long, since I've been loved."

His hands on her upper arms, he disengaged their entwined bodies, his green eyes filled with a mysterious fire Alexandria wanted to feel flickering over her naked flesh. Her breasts strained against the confines of her lacy bra. Those incredibly soft masculine hands, those fiery eyes, were taking one last impatient caress as though to break contact could possibly destroy the mood.

Pressing against him from the waist down, she silently reassured him. She wouldn't change her mind. The harsh impassioned planes of his face relaxed. Their needs were born from different causes, but were equally great.

"Come to my place . . . for the weekend?" he invited. His long tapered hands seemed unable to keep from touching her. They cupped her breasts, weighing, loving the way they nestled against his palms. His thumbs stroked the extended tips reverently.

"For the weekend? I don't have any clothes

here." She gasped, a pleasure-pain tautly scoring from her breasts to her stomach.

"Who needs clothes?" Sioux asked, grinning wickedly. "I live in an isolated area. Only the birds and flowers will see your beauty."

"You don't live in Denver?" Alex was surprised at her willingness to follow the lead of a man when she didn't even know where she was being led. *Ah, but I do know where I'm going,* she silently reflected.

Sioux shook his head negatively. "I have a place here, but I want you where the only distraction will be the need to sleep . . . from exhaustion." Alex watched as his eyes covertly scanned the room as though to regain his directional bearings.

"The delivery door is over there," she whispered in a conspiring voice.

"So it is." He chuckled. "Will you go with me?"

Alexandria laced her fingers between his. "Anywhere, anytime, any way."

CHAPTER FOUR

Sioux, in a rub-your-hands-together-anxiously mood, paced back and forth while waiting for Alexandria to throw some clothes into an overnight bag. He didn't want her to have time for introspection, but he also knew she would be damned uncomfortable if he carried her off into the sunset without a change of clothing. He didn't want her to worry about leaving her car on the company parking lot over the weekend, either. Sanity had prevailed. He had followed her back to her condo, kissed her swiftly, and made himself at home by pouring a drink.

Her place, he observed, was completely different from his own retreat. Would she walk into his mountain cabin, throw her hands in the air, and run back to civilization?

Sioux hunkered down on the leather-uphol-
stered couch, stretched his arms straight in front
of him, laced his fingers together, and popped
all ten of his knuckles. He didn't have the an-
swers to the myriad questions buzzing around in
his mind. Their going to the cabin would provide them with breathing space. The clear, crisp
air of the Rockies would clean the cobwebs from
his thinking.

"Alexandria? Get a move on it, woman," he
shouted, avoiding the question bothering him
the most. Why . . . why, knowing what he did
about Alexandria, knowing he wanted to make a
good, urbane impression on her, was he taking
her to the cabin he knew she would hate on
sight?

"I'm packing as fast as I can!" she yelled back.

What the hell did you pack for a trip when you
didn't know the destination? He'd said jeans,
shirts, and shoes. Those were neatly folded in
the bottom of the small suitcase, but they barely
took half the space. On impulse she darted into
the closet and pulled out a lovely, feminine
buttercup-yellow creation. *Who knows?* she
thought in justification as she packed it on top, *I
may need it. He may decide to have friends over
for a barbecue, or something.*

"I'm coming up there, and when I do, I seri-
ously doubt we'll be going anywhere for quite a

while," she heard him blasting from the base of the steps.

With two quick snaps Alexandria closed the lid and swung the travel bag off the bed. Heavy footfalls taking the steps two at a time could also be heard. She made it to the landing at the head of the steps at the same time he did.

One glance at the size of the suitcase and he began laughing. "You plan on taking a two-week vacation?"

"This is the smallest travel bag I own," she replied defensively, dropping it at his feet. "Ooops, I almost forgot my makeup case!" Dashing back into the bedroom she plucked the small matching case off the dresser and headed back for the door. There were absolute necessities which could not be left behind in here.

Sioux took it from her hand, bent one knee upward, and flipped the latches. "You don't need gook on your face," he said as he began emptying Beautiful Cosmetics onto a nearby table. "Ah-ha! What's this?" he asked as he dangled toward her face a package which contained a round dispenser with tiny pills.

"You're the pharmaceutical chemist—you tell me," she answered, somewhat embarrassed.

"The Pill. Prescribed for exciting, lost weekends," he analyzed with a devilish grin.

"And other things," she added. Regulating her cycle was the reason for the packet's being half-filled; otherwise she would have dumped them after her miscarriage.

Seeing the pained expression haunting her face, Sioux closed the case. For a liberated woman, he reflected, she certainly was sensitive about protecting herself from unwanted pregnancy. He tucked the boxy suitcase under his arm and draped his other arm across her shoulders. When he had seen a similar dour expression before, he had restrained himself from wiping it away with a kiss. This time there was no cause to resist the impulse. Ever so lightly he kissed her temple.

Alexandria's lips curved, the straight compressed line lifting upward. "We don't have to go anywhere, you know," she said, her honey eyes flowing toward the flowered satin coverlet on the bed.

"My invitation. My place." He led her out of the bedroom to the landing. He wanted her on his own territory. The polished prissiness of her decor made him uncomfortable.

Alex shrugged. "I guess I'm developing a case of the jitters," she explained, preceding him down the steps.

"Second thoughts? Already?"

"You'll have to admit . . . this is crazy," she replied. What had come over her? She had only met the man this morning and now she was packed and ready for a weekend in God only knew where. Unconsciously she held her breath, waiting for reassurance.

"Craziness, like beauty, is in the eye of the beholder." At the bottom of the steps he stopped. "Alexandria?" he said, his voice dropping nearly an octave. "Don't change your mind now. Please."

She pivoted on the ball of her foot to face him. "I couldn't if I wanted to, and I don't want to," she admitted honestly. Grinning impishly she added, "I was never taught to fear hell. Auntie always said she'd hate to enter the Pearly Gates and leave all her friends behind. I guess being crazy is the same way. I don't want to be sent to a booby-hatch."

"But you don't want to be left behind?" Sioux asked, returning her smile.

Alex answered by opening the front door.

* * *

Alex put her interviewing technique to good use as they drove out of the suburbs and headed in a northwesterly direction. She realized she was suffering from temporary insanity, but she wanted to know more about the man she had every intention of sharing a bed with. Her eyes glued to his chiseled profile, she picked subtly at his mind.

"Have you ever been married?" she asked after she had revealed her previous marital status.

"No. The timing was always wrong. When I had the urge, I couldn't support a wife, and when I had the money I couldn't find a woman to share it with."

"Support a wife?" she teased. "Isn't that a bit chauvinistic?"

"Hmmmm. Perhaps, but I've seen the lack of money drive couples apart. Being an only child myself, I thought I wanted a brood of 'ten little Indian boys'."

"Ten?" Alex gasped. "You don't want a wife; you want a brood mare!"

"I used the past tense. Time has managed to get away from me. I'm thirty-four and don't have the first one. But then again, if I start right away I could have a passel of kids to take care of me in my old age." He chuckled at the shocked expression on her face.

"Don't count on your brood supporting you in your old age," she commented. "You'll end up spending your retirement fund in an old folks' home."

"Wouldn't you offer your home to your parents?"

"Don't have to. Dad departed for parts unknown when I was ten, and Mom remarried a man my age last year." Alex watched the sorrowful shake of Sioux's dark head. "Don't pity me. I've coped exceedingly well."

"Fatalistically avoiding letting history repeat

itself? Or intervening by letting your career substitute for a man and a family?"

Alex scrunched down, decidedly uncomfortable with the turn of the conversation in her direction. She had trusted one man with her heart and been disillusioned. Did he think she should welcome a return bout with the fates?

"My life is stable," she answered, dodging the question.

"Sterile," Sioux muttered. "Learn from the past. Don't let it defeat you," he advised.

"Keep your pity and your words of tribal wisdom," Alex scoffed. "I don't need them." Alex turned her head away from him and stared out the side window. Moisture gathered behind her eyelids. Batting her eyes to clear away the tears, she felt them flood down her throat and swallowed convulsively.

Taking his eyes off the two-lane highway, Sioux winced at the jibe at his heritage. He noticed that when she was on the losing end of an argument, she reverted back to her scalding sarcasm to score him off. She reveled in having the last bloody word. *If the old adage "Misery loves company" is true, we should be gloriously happy*, he thought silently.

Sioux cracked his window and breathed deeply. "We're getting close to the pine forests," he said in an effort to gloss over their conflicts in values with inane conversation. Now, he belat-

70

edly realized, was not the time to settle all their personal differences.

"Are we almost there?" Alex asked, wanting to get out of the car and away from his probing questions.

"Almost. Anxious?"

"Impatient. Is your house in one of these small towns?" she asked, realizing they all had a look of sameness about them: a grocery, a post office, a gas station, and little else.

"No. My patch of land is fairly isolated. It's a welcome relief to get away from the push and pull of the city and come here."

"Aren't you bored?" Alex asked, implying her own fear. What was there to do in the middle of a forest? Pick up pine cones?

"Never," he answered. "You won't be, either," he promised. He wouldn't allow them time to be bored. He removed his right hand from the steering wheel and laid it over her hand, which was limply resting on her thigh.

The electricity conducted by the reassuring touch jolted Alex away from her discontented mood. She raised his hand and brushed her lips against it. His clean, blunt-cut fingernails, half-moon contrasting with the dark tone of his skin, was somehow comforting. Curling her fingers around his, she raked the tip of her tongue against the straight line of his forefinger nail. The soft texture of the pad gliding over her bot-

71

tom lip was a conundrum she wanted to solve. Was his secret product directly related to the condition of his skin?

"You can stop now," Sioux jokingly ordered, removing his hand from her ministrations, bracing his left foot on the floorboard as he raised his hips and adjusted his pants to accommodate the bulge she had created. His body responded instantly to her slightest touch. It was amazing to him. "A little more of that and we'll end up wrapped around a pine tree. Which is just about what I feel like right now," he murmured offhandedly.

Alex chuckled at the comparison. Her body hadn't been able to ignore the erotic sensations of having part of him inside of her, either. Maybe they were not discernible to his vision, but they were there, reminding her of the kisses they had shared, the flaming desire she had felt earlier.

Sioux turned off the highway onto a rutted side road. The interior of the car became dim as the pine trees overhead blocked the setting sun. The road wound through the forest as though the person who built the road had been more concerned with saving trees than making a direct route.

"Not a superhighway," she commented when the top of her head hit the ceiling of the car.

"Fall rains have a devastating effect on my

road. I haven't had a chance to fix it," he explained. "Usually I drive slower through here."

"Anxious?" she asked with a grin. She was redirecting at him the question he had asked her earlier.

"Noticeably," he ground out, disgusted with his lack of willpower. *Won't power,* he chastised himself. He was more than willing; it was his won't power that was sadly flagging.

"Ever made love in the front seat of a car?" she teased, leaning across the seat and running her finger with devilish delight over the flap covering his zipper.

Sioux braked the car abruptly. Turned away from the windshield, Alex braced her shoulder against the dashboard and laughed merrily.

"No, but I'm tempted." Sioux snorted, putting the car in park and flicking off the ignition. "We're here."

"Yes, we are," Alex murmured, sliding closer, fingers hopscotching up the buttons of his shirt and landing in the approximate location of the dimple she'd been unable to see during their drive.

Temptation was greater than Sioux's won't power. He gathered her against his chest with one arm as he released the button beneath the side of his seat and scooted backward, allowing room to pull her onto his lap, with both hands framing her ribcage.

Alex could feel his strong heartbeat beneath her hand; it matched the accelerated pace of her own. His eyes, dark green, matched the needles of the tall evergreens surrounding them. His fragrance was as fresh as the pine's aroma. He was an integral part of this land, she realized, as she felt the erection of his male nipples beneath her thumbs.

The slightly drooped and thickly fringed eyelashes couldn't conceal the hungry, devouring look in his eyes which communicated his savage desire to make her a part of him. Never had she felt more desirable, more beautiful, than at this suspended moment in time.

Sioux groaned, leaning back against the headrest, breaking their eye contact. "We have things to do before nightfall," he told her, wishing the modern conveniences of the city were available immediately.

Much as he needed to make love to Alexandria, he knew a city-born woman would object to the lack of water, electricity, and sheets on the bed. He was torn between passionately seducing her on the front seat, which could result in an awkward coupling, and waiting for the more fulfilling, leisurely pace of making love in the cabin. He opted for the latter and jerkily reached for the door handle.

"Get the chores done before nighttime?" Alex

taunted, disappointed in his ability to tamp his ardor.

He lifted Alexandria off his lap and practically fell out of the door with an uncharacteristic loss of balance. He righted his stooped shoulders and leaned against the cool roof of the car somewhat embarrassed by his lack of coordination. The fresh scent of the forest filled his lungs and clearing his head of Alexandria's floral bouquet, he determinedly pushed back the desire to grab her, throw her on the carpet of rusty-brown pine needles, and ravish her. Instead, he backed away from the door and extended his hand into the car's interior.

Disenchanted, Alex ignored his hand and climbed out on her own side. For Sioux's sake it was, unintentionally, the most diplomatic move she had made all day. Her jaw dropped when she saw the cabin. She had imagined a neat cottage, perhaps vine covered, or at the minimum a typical farmhouse similar to the modern versions in city suburbs. *A log cabin, for God's sake!* she silently sputtered in disbelief. She'd never seen one before, much less stayed in one.

A twig snapped behind her. Alex swirled around to find Sioux standing behind her. She could only hope the twilight shadows concealed the anguished expression on her face.

"It's not much, but it's home," Sioux offered, pride lacing through his simple statement.

"It's"—Alex searched her vocabulary for an undamning word—"interesting."

Sioux hid the smile that lurked on the corners of his mouth by swiping at it with his fingers. "Primitive?"

"Uh, interesting," she responded sincerely, not wanting to hurt his feelings. "I didn't expect a contemporary dwelling," she answered truthfully, searching again for an appropriate phrase.

"I built it myself . . . without one of those 'build your own log home' packages." Taking her elbow, he steered her toward the front porch. "See the steps? Split logs, honed to smoothness with my own hands. I even made the swing."

Alex glanced at the wooden swing barely big enough for two people to enjoy. Her eyes climbed the weathered, rusty chain, to the ceiling of the porch. Spiderwebs! She knew what that meant . . . spiders. Inwardly shuddering, she reached for the screen door; its squeaking hinges voiced the groan bubbling up from her chest.

Sioux reached around her and opened the unlocked door. "Nothing to steal," he commented at her startled expression. "Wait here. I'll get a lantern."

"A lantern?" Alex squawked. "No electricity?"

"Not that primitive. That's one of the 'chores'

76

I need to do: get the generator started, which will make power for the electric pump, which will provide you with the sweetest-tasting mountain water you'll ever have."

Skeptical that anything pumped from the ground and ingested without purification could taste good, Alex grunted. She didn't dare move in the darkness. She was certain all sorts of critters were hiding in the corners, waiting for an opportunity to crawl against her goosebumped flesh.

She heard the striking of a match and saw the rough-hewn walls of a one-room cabin and a fairly clean, orderly interior. "Nice," she said, infusing her voice with a trace of enthusiasm she didn't feel.

"Wait right here and I'll take care of the electricity," he instructed, going back out the front door and letting the screen bang closed.

Had she been fifteen years younger she would have scampered after him, clutching at his hand, refusing to be left alone in a strange place. Alex cleared her throat and nervously ran her fingers down the outside double-stitched seam of her designer jeans. She ventured a step farther into the center of the room.

"I'm bigger than you are," she muttered to any hiding vermin.

Furtively her eyes searched each corner of the cabin. She screamed involuntarily on seeing a huge shadow in one corner and hearing a screeching noise from outside.

"What the hell . . . ?" Sioux demanded, hastily pounding into the cabin, ready to protect Alex. The lights flickered, then glowed with yellow softness.

"Over there," Alex shouted, clambering into the safe haven of his open arms, and pointing blindly to the far corner.

He turned their bodies toward the corner, and when he spotted what had scared the wits out of Alexandria, he gulped down a flood of laughter. His chest heaved with suppressed mirth and his shoulders shook.

"Open your eyes, Alexandria. It's a coatrack."

Disbelieving, she peeped out, expecting a monster to lunge out and grab them both. Her knees were shaking so badly she thought she could hear them knocking together.

"Oh." She gasped, feeling decidedly foolish. Her vivid imagination had given life to the empty coat hanging limply on the rack.

"No closets," Sioux explained, straining to keep his laughter in check. He knew she was used to familiar city trappings, but he hadn't realized she was easily scared into near hysteria. "I won't let the big, bad coat get you," he teased, wrapping her trembling body back into his arms.

"Don't laugh at me," she grumbled against his chest. "What made it shout at me?"

"You probably heard the generator or the water pump," he explained, logically trying to restore reality.

"Don't leave me again, please," she beseeched sweetly. "There are other things in here that scare me silly."

"Such as?"

"Bugs, probably rats. Maybe even snakes," she threw in for good measure.

"I chemically sprayed for bugs, and the rats in the sewers of Denver would gobble up any country mouse you'd find out here."

Alex shuddered. "Snakes. What about snakes?"

"No snakes," he lied, remembering last winter when he'd opened the cabinet below the sink and found a rattler hibernating cozily in a wad of rags. He remembered having almost fainted at the realization that his hand had unknowingly run the length of it. "You're safe, Alexandria."

"Promise?" she whispered in a childlike voice. She didn't want to be a 'fraidy-cat, but she had never been in a place like this, and the unknown had a way of scaring her. At least Sioux's chest had quit shaking with laughter. It wasn't funny. Maybe, years from now, eons from now, she thought, I'll be able to look back on this and laugh. But not now. There were probably other things out there she hadn't even thought of.

"Promise," Sioux replied solemnly. "Come on, Alexandria. You're too plucky a woman to let your imagination run rampant. Look at me," he demanded softly.

Alex raised her head. "You laughed at me," she accused, doubting the sincere concern, the tenderness, she saw.

"You're a bundle of contradictions. You had no qualms about striking my face knowing I could easily break you in half, and then you practically swoon in fright when left in the dark. You're really not as tough as you'd have me believe."

A tremulous smile, shaky, but definitely a smile, creased her mouth. "Corporate dragons I can slay . . . as long as they aren't in the dark," she quipped, having regained her composure.

Sioux rewarded her bravery with a brief, hard kiss. "Want to come to the woodshed with me?"

"Tom Sawyer's dad took him to the woodshed. Am I about to be punished for my foolishness?" she teased.

"Honey, you don't in the least resemble a boy, and fatherly inclinations are the farthest thing from my mind." His hands descended to the rounded curve of her bottom, entering her back pockets and drawing her closer. "See?"

"Pine?" she laughed, twining her arms around his neck. "What do we need wood for?"

she asked, seductively rotating her hips against his pelvic bones. "I won't let you freeze."

"Lady, the only thing that kept the steering wheel out of my rump earlier was the fantasy of you stretched out on the bed . . . naked . . . arms and legs . . ."

Alex hushed his mouth with the palm of her hand. "Don't talk dirty," she warned. Blunt teeth nipped her palm and she quickly released her hold.

". . . the heat of your flesh burning against mine, allowing me to cherish you with my lips, my teeth, my tongue," he finished. "Don't confuse blatant sex with what I intend for us to share," he added, giving his own brand of warning.

"Sioux . . . kiss me. Make me believe you want more than casual sex, even if it's not true."

Their lips fused together, their eyes closed, allowing their hands and mouths to pierce through the barriers of language. Sioux realized she had fears far deeper, far more serious than being afraid of the dark. He used his lips to convince her of a truth her words had instantly revealed to him. He was falling in love with her.

His body had instinctively known, from the first kiss, that she was special, but he had denied his instincts. Physical attraction was not equatable with love. Lust wasn't love. Remembering the cruel verbal blows he had flung at her made him tremble with remorse. He wanted to tell her of his discovery, his love, but knew she wouldn't believe him. It was too soon. Empty words, spoken from a forked tongue, was how she would perceive and reject a declaration of love.

CHAPTER FIVE

Sioux knew the passage of time held the single clue as to how and when to tell Alexandria. He also knew their time for physical love was right. *To deny her, to deny myself, release from this torment would be criminal neglect.*

Nimble fingers flew down the front of Sioux's shirt. Alexandria undid the buttons quickly, as though to delay might make the feat impossible. His chest was smooth, almost hairless. A gold chain with a dangling turquoise emblem contrasted with the teak color and the polished texture. The smoothness of his chest reminded her of expensive wood. Her arms splayed the shirt apart, tugging it loose from his slacks and then wrapping themselves around his waist. When he turned, she discovered the same perfection in the skin tones covering the supple, flexing muscles between his shoulder blades.

The passion unlike any she had ever felt began burning a path from her head, to her heart, to her stomach, to the core of her feminine being. Or was it the skimming touch of Sioux's hand tracing languid circles from the crown of her head to her hips which instigated the sensation? She didn't know. Didn't care. The combustion caused by his mere touch brought to life every passionate cell in her wanton body.

She felt his thumb beneath the flap of her zippered jeans slowly climbing and descending tooth by tooth across her belly, his fingertips exploring the curve of her hipbone, the heel of his hand preceding the torturous path of his thumb. Parting her jean-clad thighs, she willed him to make a more intimate exploration. Alexandria couldn't keep the sigh of joy behind her lips when he followed the double-stitched seam downward, rubbing, applying pressure as it reached the cross seam. Her dark golden eyes opened and found Sioux staring, the stark planes of his face harsh, intent on the dewiness of her lips and, she was certain, the intimate dewiness desire had drenched his fingertip with.

"Want me?" she asked huskily, needing to hear the deep lullaby of his voice.

"All of you," he throatily answered, revolving the heel of his hand, imitating the fantasy of his pelvis grinding against her in the throes of love. His knees nearly buckled when her hand cupped him through the lightweight fabric of his slacks. The light stroke, a blend of timidity and boldness, broke his control.

"Harder," he gasped, using all ten fingers to shakily, clumsily unbutton her blouse, remove it, fling it aside.

He paused, cupping the underside curve of her hardening breasts. Feeling the pressure building in his loins, he knew her passionate exploration would lead to unfulfilled passion if he didn't stop her thumb from raking over the supersensitive length of his manhood. With the willpower of ten men he slipped one arm behind her back, the other behind her knees, and lifted her, cradled her, as he strode lazily to the unmade bed.

Alexandria's equilibrium was lost. When Sioux carefully, gently, laid her on the bed, every bone in her body felt limp, fluid. The coarse ticking of the mattress scratched her back, contrasting with the smoothness of Sioux's hands as he unsnapped her jeans, hooked his thumbs at the waistband, and very slowly and lingeringly pulled them off and cast them carelessly aside.

"You're what every man dreams of," he told her in a hushed voice. "Your skin is as pale as the color of your hair." Using the side of his small finger he traced the path of the sun mark left by the bikini bottom she'd worn weeks ago. "I'm jealous of the sun kissing your skin before I did," he whispered, his eyes scorching a heated journey as it followed his finger over the white line of demarcation.

"I want to lovingly kiss the parts of you even the sun was denied," he rasped huskily as his fingers combed through the fluff shielding her womanhood. "Golden, darker than the sun-streaked hair," he whispered aloud, watching it cling to his fingers.

"No," Alexandria gasped. "Not there."

Sioux's hand left a burning sensation tingling her skin as he silently obeyed her command, drowsily moving to the rosebud tips of her breasts, which were also untanned by the sun.

"I can wait. I'm very patient," he temporarily acquiesced. "But not for this."

"Not yet, Sioux," Alexandria gasped, protectively crossing her chest with her arms. "I want to see you. I want to feel you beside me."

She feared his slow loving ministrations would burn her insides into cinders and ashes before they had reached the ultimate ecstasy if she wasn't allowed to feel the cool suppleness of his body against hers.

Sioux nodded, again agreeing to her demands. Without haste he unhooked his beltless slacks, unzippered them, and let them fall in a heap to the floor. The muted glow of the lantern on the table cast a yellow sheen on his bronze skin. His tumescent manhood strained against the confining bounds of his dark briefs. Confidently he peeled his remaining garment off and stood proudly before her.

Alexandria reached toward him, eager to touch him.

"No." Sioux groaned, denying what he wanted, but knowing the pace of their lovemaking needed to be slowed down rather than accelerated. If she touched him, he'd explode.

Lying down beside her, turning her on her side, putting his arms beneath her, he was content to feel the softness of her body against him.

"Sioux? Are you torturing me on purpose?" Alexandria asked, bewildered by his platonic hold.

"Myself," he groaned in reply. "Just let me hold you for a moment until I get a grip on myself."

Alexandria grinned, feeling the tenseness of his jaw matching the tautness of the muscles in his thighs. "I'd rather be the one with the grip," she teased huskily, easing her head away from him.

Sioux chuckled, praying the light banter would cool his ardor enough for him to make their loving good for her. "I'm theoretically opposed to the All-American quickie."

"You've been making love to me since this

afternoon with your eyes, your hands, your mouth, haven't you? How much foreplay do I have to tolerate?"

Groaning, Sioux draped his leg around her thighs, drawing her closer until he nestled in her golden triangle. "If I die, right now, I'll be buried where I belong."

"Don't you dare die!" Alexandria emphatically whispered, biting his neck above the jugular vein in a vampish manner.

"Why not? I've never been this close to heaven."

Alexandria strung a nipping row of kisses down his neck to his collarbone. She felt Sioux's soft masculine hands coming to life as he began massaging her back, slipping to her breast, gently squeezing, rolling her engorged nipple between thumb and forefinger, creating a shaft of pleasure-pain that made her gulp air into her lungs.

"Will your breasts taste as sweet as your lips?" Sioux asked.

"Better," Alexandria promised, luring him, enticing him, by twisting her torso until both her shoulders were touching the mattress.

Sioux delightedly accepted the invitation. Gently turning the lower half of her body, resting between her thighs, his bent elbows balancing his weight, he nuzzled one, then the other.

"You smell like a spring bouquet. Let me taste

you," he whispered, lowering his head, circling the dark aureoles with his flattened tongue. "Luscious."

"Stop playing," Alexandria groaned. "Take me into your mouth. God, I feel like I'm on fire."

The wetness of his tongue didn't extinguish the flames; it brought the fire roaring to life as though fanned by the air in his lungs. He sipped each tip, his teeth fanning the red-orange flames behind her closed eyelids. Alexandria arched her hips against his waist with each sensuous pull.

"Exciting, exquisite torture. Give me more," she pleaded softly, panting the words out from her soul.

Dragging his torso upward with unexpected strength, Alexandria blindly sought his lips. She suckled his ravaging tongue with the same mastery he had used on her breasts. Her knees pressed on each side of his hips, urging him to put an end to her suffering. He refused by pushing one slender leg down and moving across it.

Mewing sounds of frustration followed her seeking tongue as she darted it beside his, entering, thrusting into him savagely. She jerked shakily, convulsively, when she felt his hand once again parting the soft satin-slick petals of her womanhood, dipping intimately inside, matching the stroking of her tongue with his finger.

Alexandria silently taught him her preferences as she circled her tongue, quickly darting in and out, pressing against the roof of his mouth, receiving and echoing pressure. She was mindlessly leading him on to her own downfall. The muted masculine groans she heard as she flicked the inner rim of his lips were her single means of knowing Sioux was thoroughly aroused, wanted release from his own building frustration.

"Take me, now," she whispered hungrily, lips moving against his, soft inner thighs clamping against his hand. "Now or never," she threatened.

Sioux crossed back between her thighs as though meekly obeying her command.

"You could refuse me? Now?" He groaned, nuzzling his manhood against the gates of his own heaven. "Can you?"

"Yes, damn you," she cursed in frustration. "No," she capitulated humbly when she felt him withdrawing. "I think I'll die of wanting if you don't love me."

Sioux pierced her like an arrow in slow motion. He couldn't contain the quick intake of air as he felt her stretch and claim him in a liquid fieriness. The shaft of the arrow sank deeper, seeking the source of the fire until the feathers, his own dark hair, kissed the golden gates. Teeth clenched, he didn't know if he would ever in this lifetime be able to move away from the heavenly sensation of being inside of Alexandria.

He could hear the faint tom-tom beat of primitive drums, his own heartbeat, setting the rhythm of his thrusting hips. Green eyes open, watching the flickering smile on Alexandria's lips, he knew they were sharing utopia. Plunging deeper into a timeless state, he heard her chanting his name. Saw her lips lovingly purse with each stroke. He knew it couldn't last, wouldn't last, forever, but, oh, God he wanted it to.

"Sioux . . . Sioux," Alexandria panted, spiraling toward ecstasy.

She could feel the muscles in his biceps tensing with each thrust. Could feel herself tensing as though preparing for a mighty leap toward ultimate fulfillment. Slumberously she opened her eyes. She needed to see the face of the man, the only man, who was responsible for the joy pumping through her veins. Unable to contain it, she felt the joy erupt within her, and her eyes closed and a flush crept from within her body, swathing her chest with a rosy glow.

Sioux knew he had taken Alexandria over the threshold of ecstasy and could no longer restrain himself from catapulting, spilling his seed, calling her name with each throbbing spurt of masculine essence. He had given all of himself for her safekeeping.

"You made the reward greater than the price of the torture," Alexandria whispered when their breathing had approached normalcy. "You're wonderful."

Sioux rolled to his side and pulled her with him. "There are a million things I want to say," he confided, "but you sapped my strength and in my weakness I'm afraid of saying the wrong thing."

Rocking her head negatively on the arm beneath her hair, she denied the possibility of his being able to say or do anything wrong. "Say them," she encouraged.

"Do you believe in love at first sight?" he asked recklessly.

"A long, long time ago I did, but I think I gave up on the idea. Why?"

"I'm not certain I believed it possible, either. I've wanted women . . . been with other women, but it's as though they were practice sessions which prepared me for you," he whispered pensively.

"Experience being the best teacher?" she probed.

"Mmmm-hmmmm, something like that. Was what I experienced one sided or did you feel it, too?" he asked with trepidation.

Alexandria paused to think about his question.

In their loverlike embrace, in their hushed tones, was he saying the words he really felt? Or was this just small talk? Propping herself up on one elbow she pushed against his shoulder until he lay flat on the bed. He seems sincere, she thought, her eyes sweeping over his sculptured features. For some unknown reason she knew he was as vulnerable emotionally as she was.

"I've been married," she admitted thoughtfully. When she saw his brow pucker she reached up and smoothed it with her fingers. "And betrayed," she tacked on, informing Sioux of her divorced status. "My love barometer is lousy. You could be leading me up a rose-strewn path with a funeral pyre at the end, and I wouldn't know it."

"I'm not," he vowed. "I wouldn't do anything intentionally to hurt you. You mean too much to me."

Her fingertip followed the natural part of his hair to the crown, tousling the thickness into further disorder. "Men baffle me," she confessed. "I don't understand their ability to say they love a woman and still be out in the field hunting for other unwary game."

"Do you think all men are without honor?" Sioux asked, dreading her answer.

"Statistically men can be classified into two categories: those chasing skirts and those who

93

wish they could. That's why the divorce rate is soaring."

"And I suppose you neatly tucked me in the first slot?" he asked levelly, with a tight control on his inflection.

"You aren't married. I'd worry if you hadn't had past affairs," she answered drily. Smoothing her hands over his high cheekbones, she laughed huskily. "Unless of course you're an escapee from a monastery."

"Of the three choices I think I prefer the last." Sioux paused, knowing he could never break a vow, not even one of celibacy if that was what he believed in. Sacred vows weren't to be violated. "On second thought," he corrected, "I'm not a man who makes vows lightly. When I decide to marry it will be for keeps."

"I've heard that promise before."

"But not from me. A promise made is a promise kept," he retorted forcefully.

"Don't make any promises to me, then. I truly believe I would go crazy if I trusted a man again and discovered he was a louse."

"Do you realize you're equating the entire male species with one blood-sucking louse?" he asked, questioning her logic, the strength of belief behind her statement.

Alexandria laughed aloud. "That is going a bit overboard, isn't it?"

"More than a bit," he pressed, wanting her to

have a clearer understanding of her false belief. Gently he used one finger to traverse the hollow of her throat. "Would you believe a vow if I made it?"

"That tickles," she protested, brushing his hand away.

"Don't change the subject. Would you?" he repeated, determined to get an honest answer from her.

Her honey-sweet eyes flowed over his face, searching for signs of hidden deceit, and found none. Did she trust him? she wondered. Decidedly more important, could she trust him? In the warm intimacy of his arms she wanted to. She realized it would be wonderful to hear a vow of eternal love, but she knew, deep in her heart, that she wouldn't believe it. They would be words springing up from the well of passion and she certainly wouldn't be naive enough to believe them.

"No vows or promises," she insisted. "Without lies there is no pain. This . . . combustion between us may wear off. I don't want to leave my heart behind as a charred remain, okay?"

"I can hear your tears, Alexandria. My body flinches from your pain, but I can't promise not to fall in love with you. To do so would truly be a lie."

Alexandria felt his disappointment in her answer but couldn't change the course of her life;

however, she decided she could change the topic. "I'm hungry. Does the stove over there work?"

"Are you really hungry for food?" Sioux asked, disliking her ability to switch from the important to the mundane.

"Yep," she declared. Rolling off the bed she fluidly pulled on her jeans, picked up her bra and shirt, and began dressing.

Resigned to postponing any further serious conversation, Sioux rose from the bed and pulled on his own clothing. "The groceries are in the car. Don't wear your bra."

The two completely unrelated thoughts stopped Alexandria's arms just as she was looping them through the bra straps. "What?"

"Don't wear your bra . . . please," he repeated slowly a little louder.

"I won't be comfortable without it." She reached behind herself to put the hooks into the eyes.

"Please?" Sioux requested. "I'd rather watch you in this natural setting completely au naturel, but I'm willing to compromise."

"You're a hard man to refuse," Alexandria softly answered as she complied with his entreaty. She then buttoned her shirt from top to bottom.

"I'll trade you one fantastic dinner for the permanent removal of your bra," he bartered.

"Who cooks? The chief or the squaw?" She winked broadly at him as she watched him shrug into his shirt.

"No hard and fast rules in this teepee," he tossed back. "You can cook, can't you?"

"I'm a whiz in the kitchen. Bring on the frozen food and I'll get the oven and the boiling water ready," she kidded, laughing at his grimacing face.

"In that case, I'll cook; you clean up," he countermanded as he shoved his feet into his shoes.

"No way. You'll probably dirty every pot and plate in the kitchen and I'll have dishpan hands before the weekend is over."

"I can take care of the dishpan hands." He chuckled. "But I refuse to corrode my stomach with processed food."

"You aren't a natural-food freak, are you?" she demanded, stomach growling at the thought of eating nuts and fruit for two days. "Remember the slogan," she lightly teased: "You are what you eat."

"Wait and see" was his mysterious reply. He opened the door and strode out toward the car.

Alex breathed a sigh of relief as she emptied the two grocery bags while Sioux put the goods away. Meat, potatoes, vegetables, fruit, brought chuckles as she handed them to him. Normal food for normal people, she thought gratefully.

"Want to grill the steaks?" he asked as he dug

a bag of charcoal from beneath the stainless steel sink.

"While you fix the salad?" she quipped, knowing he was asking preference, not who was to do what.

Hands on his hips in mock anger, he let out a low murderous growl. "I eat my meat raw!"

"In that case, you can do both." She laughed. "But for me, I think I'll at least warm mine on the outside. Where's the barbecue pit?"

"Outside," he quipped smugly, "with all the creatures of the wild who are waiting for a delectable bite of your luscious . . ." The fear entering her eyes made him stop, reach for her, and fold her into his arms. "I was teasing. Come on. You're perfectly safe. I won't let anything hurt you."

"That has all the markings of a weak promise. What happens if a humongous bear is hiding in the trees out there?"

"I'll wrestle it like they do in the movies. But don't be disappointed at the lack of bears within a thousand miles."

"Alligators?"

"Maybe a harmless lizard."

"Vampire bats?"

"Plain old wing-flapping variety here."

"The Abominable Snowman?"

"The Loch Ness monster?" he quipped, adding to the list of improbable inhabitants for a Rocky Mountain retreat.

"Hmmmm. Dracula?"

"I'm going to suck your blood!" he teased, pretending to mark a spot on her delectable neck.

Alexandria arched one eyebrow and pushed at his chest. "And I'm going to let you." Laughing, totally unafraid of the villainous leer on his face, she walked toward the door. "You're completely harmless," she goaded, wanting him to follow her outside just in case she did need protection from the unknown.

Sioux scooped up the charcoal bag and followed her. He honestly hoped their light-hearted banter had banished her fear of nature, but realized it hadn't. With a wry twist of his lips he conceded that Alexandria was out of her element, both outside and inside the cabin. She knew as little about love, true love, as she did about the beauty of being at harmony with the great out-of-doors.

"It's dark out here," Alex complained as she stuck her hand in front of her face, barely able to see it.

"No city lights, but wait until I show you the stars," he reassured her. "Take a deep breath. Listen to the night noises."

"Don't hear a thing," she perversely argued.

"Your eyes and ears will adjust in a while. By Sunday you'll dread going back to Denver."

Alexandria's eyes did adjust, she could hear the crickets chirping and the soft sighing of the pine needles as the night breeze gently blew through the trees. Pleasant, she mused, sucking a lungful of air between her teeth, but strange. Chuckling to herself, she began humming one of her mother's favorite Broadway songs: "Take my hand . . . I'm a stranger in paradise."

CHAPTER SIX

Alex smiled to herself as she leaned back in her cane-backed chair and watched Sioux finish up the dishes. He certainly didn't have any hang-ups about role reversals. When she had suggested sharing the task of cleaning up, he had laughed, swatted her rump as she leaned over to clear the table, and firmly told her he didn't want "prune-skinned" hands marring his back. Glancing at her perfectly manicured fingernails, which hadn't washed dishes for years, then glancing at the mound of frothy bubbles in the sink, she almost wished she had insisted on volunteering.

Watching his quick efficient movements, Alexandria found herself mesmerized by the competency of the man she had started the day hating and ended the day . . . *Don't even think it,* she warned herself dourly. *This is too soon; too fast to last.*

The gurgling of water draining out of the sink and Sioux's snatching off the dishtowel he'd tucked into his waistband brought her out of her reverie. Reaching under the cabinet Sioux extracted a white pharmaceutical bottle, twisted off the lid, and poured a creamy white lotion into the palm of his hand as he turned around and faced her.

"Want some?" he offered.

"Is this what keeps your hands so soft? What is it?" she asked, taking the unlabeled plastic container from his hand.

"Nothing you'll find on the market." He rubbed the lotion into the skin on the back of his hands.

"A secret product?" She remembered him mentioning that he'd developed a revolutionary product.

"There are a multitude of good hand creams on the market," he responded, dodging her question.

"Oh, no, you don't," she said as she slammed the front legs of the chair down and grabbed his arm. "You're evading the question. Is this your miracle product?"

"No. Keep the bottle if you like and have it analyzed. There are no secret ingredients . . .

no magic potions." The dimple Alex had grown to love popped in and out as he smiled, and then frowned. "Playing Mata Hari?"

"Prying information out of the enemy with seduction?" she asked, false sweetness coating the pain his covert implication had caused.

Does he think I slept with him to get a damned formula? she fumed silently. *He must think I'm lower than any creepy crawly bug. Does he think I'm unscrupulous, without integrity?*

"No, Alexandria. Using your body would be too high a price for you to pay. This afternoon I might have conjectured about that possibility, but not now." He pulled her rigid form against his chest, smoothing the flaxen hair from her neck downward. "Don't ask me to reveal what I think will cause a dramatic change in the glamor industry," he murmured against the sensitive skin at her hairline. "I'd tell you, but I'd hate myself Monday."

"Why? You'll have to tell us sooner or later if we hire you."

The husky laugh beside her ear made her spine tingle. Relaxing against his hard body, she raised her face, wanting to end the conversation, wanting to be kissed senseless rather than discuss the boardroom politics they'd be facing Monday.

"You'll be the first to know whether you hire

103

me or not," he whispered before lightly brushing her lips with his own.

"I like the way you kiss," she complimented him, grateful for his willing interest in her as a woman rather than as an executive. "It's a lost art form."

"I fed your stomach; you feed my ego by explaining what you mean," he coaxed.

"Well . . . remember when you kissed me the first time?"

"Um-hmm," he distractedly responded as he lightly brushed his lips down the hollow under her cheekbone.

"You didn't French."

"What?" he hooted in disbelief as he drew back, laughing.

"You didn't French-kiss me. Your lips were closed."

Completely disarmed by her disclosure, Sioux couldn't do anything but chuckle and marvel at her admission.

"Why is it nine of ten men consider it their duty to stick their tongue in where it doesn't belong?" she quizzed, keeping a straight face, although his laughter was delightfully infectious.

"As mad as you were, I'd have been missing the tip and speaking with a lisp had I been that audacious. I'm certain I'll lose my toenail as it is!"

104

Alex could no longer restrain herself from laughing. "Did I really hurt you?"

"Want to see?" he asked sultrily, turning, leading her to the low couch in front of the fireplace.

"I'll kiss it better," she outlandishly offered.

"The day I see you on bended knee, kissing my feet, is the day the sky falls in. I'll settle for having you kiss my lips, but first I'm going to get a fire going."

"You're a romantic at heart, aren't you?" she asked as she curled up on one end of the sofa, stretching her legs and then tucking them next to her bottom.

Sioux's eyes had never left her. He enjoyed watching her uninhibited, graceful movements. He'd seen a kitten sleepily follow the same routine. He wondered if Alexandria would purr with contentment. The magic of the cabin was subtly working on her, too. She was gradually relaxing, dropping her guard. Somehow he doubted she had ever discussed kissing techniques with any other man. The thought pleased him.

"Aren't you?" Alex repeated, a heated flush following the path his dazzling green eyes made as she anticipated his hands rediscovering her flesh.

"Probably," he agreed. "Why you'd think so, though, I can't imagine." Turning away from her he began building the fire by twisting newspaper, then meticulously pyramiding six small logs on the grate. "How romantic was I when I practically ripped your clothes off and flung you on an unmade bed?" Sioux exasperatedly shook his head as he struck a wooden match and stuck it below the paper.

Alex laughed throatily. "I didn't notice at the time, but I guess you were a real brute," she teased.

The small flame of the match ignited the paper and quickly spread to encompass the outer bark of the logs. *The logs and I have something in common,* Sioux realized. *Both of us will be burning out of control very shortly.* He couldn't stop the wildfire any more than the logs could.

"I can't deny it," he concurred, swiveling at the waist to see if she was smiling. "I noticed you made the bed while I was outside grilling the steaks."

"Self-preservation. My back will be as sore as your toe."

Sioux pulled the screen in front of the open fire, then straightened and lazily crossed to stand in front of Alex. "Scoot to the center."

"Why?" she asked. She watched him walk toward the table they had eaten on, pick up the container of lotion, and turn off the light before returning to the couch.

"Never mind," he said, sitting on the opposite end and spreading his legs apart. "Turn around,

106

scoot up against me, and I'll put some of this on your back. It has aloe in it and should soothe away any discomfort."

"I was kidding," she averred, but followed his directions anyway.

Sioux lifted the back of her blouse and inspected the alabaster skin carefully. There were light scratches in several places. "I'm sorry," he apologized, feeling every bit as brutish as she had accused him of being. "I think I'd better have you take your top off. I don't want the oil in this to stain your blouse."

"You'd better take your shirt off, too," she suggested. "I don't want your clothes stained, either." Alexandria heard the rustle of cloth being removed and smiled. What a delightful way of getting rid of cumbersome garments. "Do you think I ought to take my jeans off, too?"

"Not if you want this rubbed on your back! Lean forward," he instructed when she had removed her blouse.

Moving her long length of hair over her shoulder, he dribbled a squirt between her shoulder blades, put the bottle down, and began stroking the warm lotion into the pores of her skin. "Feel good?" he asked when he heard her moan.

"Um-hmmm. You have the softest hands."

"Thank you, m'lady."

Neither of them spoke as each enjoyed the feel of the other. The crackling of the fire as wood sap heated and exploded was the only noise accompanying the low groans of enjoyment coming from Alexandria.

"The fire smells good, doesn't it?" she said lazily.

"Almost as good as the fresh sunshine smell of your hair," he answered, softly wiping his hands on his jeans and lifting the vibrant living sunshine off her shoulders. "You've never had it cut, have you?"

"Uh-uh. I should. Most of the time it's a pain. It takes forever to dry."

"You don't blow-dry it. I can almost see you sitting in the sun letting it feather through your fingers. It's"—he let a silvery strand slide over his palm, kissing his lifeline—"breathtaking."

Alex leaned back, loving the feel of her hair between his chest and her back, then flushed when she realized her breasts were taut, easily viewable. A sharp shudder coursed through her when Sioux's hands inched around her waistband and at a snail's pace touched the skin warmed by the fire. When had she ever been so immodest? she asked herself. Never, came a ready reply.

"Do you like working for an exclusively female corporation?" Sioux asked in an attempt to master his desire to taste what his hands were touching. He was dangerously close to losing control and it made him disgusted with himself.

They needed to talk more than they needed to renew their carnal knowledge of each other, he reminded himself. Alexandria squirmed closer, swishing her hair beneath his nose, and wiggled her bottom snugly against the crotch of his pants. Gritting his teeth, stoically determined not to grope and grab again, he squeezed his eyes closed.

"I guess," Alex answered when she was settled close enough to twist her neck and be able to see his face. "I was pregnant when Jane hired me," she confided.

"You don't have any children," he remarked unthinkingly.

"How do you know?"

He couldn't tell her how he knew she was childless any more than he could explain her name printed on the placard he'd carried. Part of the promise he'd made entailed not revealing the source until he was hired and his product marketed.

"You'd be too good a mother to waltz off for the weekend without making explicit arrangements for your child, wouldn't you?"

"I wouldn't be here if I had a child," she corrected. "Anyway," she continued, "Jane has become my mentor, and my friend. My job is exciting because of all the awards she's been given . . . and being in on the marketing of products

109

is intriguing. Basically, I guess I'm fairly content with my life."

"Do you date?"

"Not often. What about yourself?"

"Growing up as an only child made me pretty much a loner."

"How did you get into the pharmaceutical business?" she asked, disinclined to probe into the number of women, how often, where, did he love any of them, as though to know would cause infinite pain.

"You do that a lot, you know?" he whispered huskily.

"What?"

"Avoid getting to the root of a problem."

"I know. It's a safety device. If you don't ask, you don't get hurt," she confided, lolling her head back against his shoulder. "I'm jealous of every woman you've ever touched, held, wanted . . ." Her eyes rolled backward as she said each word, until they were closed.

Excluding the sorrow in her words, the thought of Alexandria caring enough to admit jealousy sent Sioux into euphoric flight. He knew she wasn't the bed-hopping, sleep-around type, but it thrilled him to know the chemistry between them had a steadier base. They weren't building on the shifting, temporary foundation of lust.

"Don't be," he reassured her. "Do you really want to know why I became a chemist?"

Her head rocked affirmatively, sensuously tugging the blanket of silky hair against his heated chest. "Lean forward a moment," he gently commanded when he saw her brow wince. Parting her hair in the back, he lifted one side of it over her shoulder, then the other, spreading it over her chest as though it were a lightweight blanket which would keep them both warm. "Better?"

"Hmmmmm."

"I've always been curious about why old folk-remedies worked. Why does spreading a spider's web over an abrasion speed the healing process? Why do herbal teas give relief to a severe cold? Why does aloe make the pain of a burn magically disappear? A thousand and one whys made me curious. No one could explain where I grew up, and believe it or not, when I went to college most of the professors didn't know, either. Didn't know, or didn't care," he amended. "For a while I was caught up in their 'chemical solutions' to every human disorder until . . ." Sioux stopped. He was dangerously close to disclosing his personal vow. A pledge of absolute silence for fear of retribution made him bite his tongue.

"Until?" Alex prompted.

"Someone asked me why man could keep

111

dead skin, leather, supple, but couldn't keep live skin from becoming wrinkled, spotted, and dry."

Alex interrupted, "And that's when you switched from the whys of healing to the whys of the glamor industry?"

"More or less. Working with internally ingested drugs can be frustrating with a capital F. It's only been in the past year that legislation has made producing drugs in small quantities for people with rare diseases profitable. It's damned discouraging to know the cure and have a manufacturing company say, 'Sorry, we can't make money producing it.' Hell, if it keeps some human being from suffering, how can they *not* produce it?"

A tightening of his lips, his heavy sigh, indicated his vain attempt to justify in his mind the materialistic viewpoint of those people responsible for company policy.

"Then there's the years of testing it takes to get a miracle drug on the market. It's . . . frustrating," he reemphasized.

Alex raised the dark golden fringe of eyelash. She saw the frustration he had spoken of clearly etched on his face. "You really care, don't you?"

"Yes," he succinctly replied. "Too much."

"Never too much. The 'me society' of the sixties is supposed to be dead, but it flourishes under the guise of private enterprise. I'm glad you care; I'm glad you told me."

Using two fingers, she stretched his mouth upward at the tips into the facsimile of a smile. He immediately responded by taking her wrist, raising her palm, placing a moist kiss on the fleshy pad beneath her thumb, then wrapping her fingers over it as though doing so would keep it there forever.

"Heavy stuff. A waste of the mood I created with the glowing fire and the body massage," he derided as he uncurled her hand and flattened it over her heart. "My intent was to listen to you rather than bore you to tears."

She hadn't noticed the glimmering brightness clinging precariously to her eyelashes until he brought it to her attention. She had felt her soul weeping for the people in pain he had futilely tried to reach, for the idealism she knew had been shattered when he was a young man, for . . . the tenderness of the kiss he had carried to her heart. *He's noble, majestic, a strong man,* she admired silently.

"I'm shedding the tears you aren't able to," she whispered, laying her cheek against his for him to share their soothing dampness.

"Men cry," he hoarsely corrected. "When I'm outside walking in the woods and a butterfly lights on my shoulder, or when the angry clouds of a storm clear and the pure colors of a rainbow arch against their grayness, their beauty brings tears to my eyes. When I see you stretched out, relaxed, beautiful, at peace with yourself and me, it brings unmanly tears to my eyes. I conceal them; swallow them back; men aren't supposed to weep."

"What a shame," she consoled. "I've shed buckets of tears. Wasted them on things far less valuable. Beauty brings tears to your eyes; pain brings them to mine." Slowly, tenderly, with a depth of feeling she didn't understand, she turned and kissed him, parting her lips for him to taste the tears she, too, had unconsciously swallowed.

CHAPTER SEVEN

Alexandria was content with the passionless kiss. Her heart was singing a languorous hymn whose sweet lyrics promised a greater quantity of loving than a mortal woman deserved. Sioux had trusted her with a glimpse of himself she was confident he had never shared. Unprotected, he had symbolically held his secret thoughts out to her for her examination. She could have laughed at his dreams and his impractical view of the world. Could have cut him down with one fell blow by scoffing at his admission of tears. She didn't, couldn't, any more than she could harm the fragile bond of trust entwining them together.

Protectively she cradled his head in her arms as she mutely told him of the gratitude she felt for being allowed to go past the bounds of physical attraction. She was not a person who normally let desire or lust rule her head or her heart. Perhaps, she thought, there is something to the old idea of finding one's lost soul mate. Could she forget past hurts, past betrayals of trust and love, and begin again? Could she finally let down her guard and be as open and frank as Sioux had been? Fear of being hurt again made her decide against impetuosity.

For endless moments they clung to each other silently, basking in the warmth of the fire, and the close relationship they were developing. Alex wondered if friendship with a person of the opposite sex was possible. Was liking a man imperative before falling in love? At eighteen the thought had never entered her mind. Getting married after graduation from high school was what her mother and her friends had expected. Getting pregnant right away was the next step. She admitted her own immaturity was an underlying factor in her having allowed others to dominate and lead her around by the nose. This was no longer true, she fervently hoped as she buffed her hair against the sparse hair on Sioux's chest. It had taken years of insulating herself from harm by working in an all-female environment, but Sioux was opening the soft cocoon. The tingling response she felt when he touched her from waist to shoulder, from shoulder to hip, was more than the awakening of the flesh; it was an awakening from an eight-year protective nap.

The time for reflective thought ended when Sioux sat up, lifting Alex with him, cradling her against him as he carefully lowered both of them to the braided rug in front of the hearth.

"Tired?" he asked when he saw her stretch, delicately covering a yawn with her hands.

Alex smiled lazily, watching him as he first shed his jeans, then removed hers. "Do you plan to add more scratches to my back?" she kidded lightly.

Sioux sat back on his haunches, watching the glow from the fire splay across her pale skin. It gave the illusion of flames licking her, tasting her sweetness, discovering and enveloping a beauty which rivaled its own. He couldn't resist following the flow of the flames. Gingerly he stroked from her kneecap, up the creamy softness of her thighs, to her waist, over the indentation between her hipbones, across the shadowed crevices between her ribs, on to the darkness beneath her breasts.

"Have you ever made love in front of a fire?" he asked softly.

"Never," she replied, mesmerized by the concentric circles he was weaving, and the reflective glow of the fire in his eyes as he rhythmically followed its course.

"Would you be more comfortable in the bed?" he asked, showing concern for the scratches on her back.

"No," she whispered. His fingers simultaneously circled both her nipples. She raised her hands and gripped the corded muscles below his elbow, drawing him closer. "With the fire behind you, you look like a pagan god about to teach a maiden about the glories of love. Teach me, Sioux. Teach me, now."

As Sioux made love to her with slow deliberation, he prayed he was teaching her about love. He worshiped her with his hand and lips. She was the goddess; he was the pagan god. He smiled when she raked her feminine claws over his shoulders and back, making her mark on him. There was no pain, only the wonder of knowing they had passed the brink of consciously trying to please each other and had gone on to a compelling need for ecstatic fulfillment.

When she arched beneath him, embracing him deep within, he silently shouted her name, silently proclaimed his love for the enchanting goddess who was afraid to declare hers. He knew he had taught her to share the joys of loving, but also knew she had a long way to go before she would understand the value of being at one with herself, with nature . . . and with him.

Midnight had come and gone without Sioux's obtaining a promise of employment. But he'd made other silent promises regarding Alexandria. The newspaper would hit the stands; he would be employed by Lady Jane, and then . . . For the first time he doubted that the means of attaining his goal had justified the end result.

Alex momentarily didn't know where she was or how she had come to be there when she awakened. Not my bed, she thought fragmentedly, realizing it was softer than her usual firm mattress. Eyes closed, she instantly remembered the events of the previous day and night. A smile tugged her lips upward. Had anyone recited them she would have scoffed at the improbability of Alexandria Foster's being whisked away from the comfortable safety of Denver and Beautiful Cosmetics by a man she had called Ms. Sioux. Mentally she strung out the long vowel sound of his name until it rhymed with *coo*. She remembered having fallen asleep to the lullaby of Sioux's crooning her name. It had been wonderful. He had been wonderful. Grinning wider, she thought, *I was wonderful!*

"Lazybones, sleepin' in the sun, How you gonna get a day's work done?" Sioux sang from outside the screen door.

"I'm on temporary vacation. I don't have to get up, do I?" she asked, propping herself up on

119

both elbows with complete disregard for the effect gravity was having on the top sheet.

Sioux slapped his forehead as though pounding into his head the thought of her being in his bed all day. His hand raked through his wet hair to smooth back his errant forelock.

"You have five minutes to get out of bed. The demons of lust are warring in my chest and I can only fight them for"—he glanced at his watch—"four and a half more minutes."

"Who wants to fight?" Alex teased, crooking her finger in his direction.

"Alexandria," he warned in a growling tone, "get out of the bed."

"Uh-uh," she sultrily replied. "I guess this is your way of telling me that in the light of day . . . you don't respect me anymore."

"Alexandria," he growled louder, opening the screen and charging into the small room.

"Whaaaaaat?" she asked coyly, her voice swinging upward.

"I'm going to tickle you right out of that bed if you don't get moving," he threatened.

Alex smiled as she bluffed, "I'm not ticklish."

Lifting the sheet and blanket from off the bottom of the bed, Sioux's hand snaked in and grabbed her ankle. One finger went from the tip of her big toe downward. By the time he touched the ball of her foot she was wiggling and shrieking, and by the time he went from the arch to the heel, she was kicking, trying to break his hold.

"Not ticklish, huh?" he chuckled, scrabbling up and down her foot with featherlike strokes.

"Okay, I give up!" She laughed. "Let me up!"

"This little piggy went to market," he began, thumb and forefinger on her big toe. "This little piggy stayed home."

"I won't stay home. I'll get up," she promised, curling her toes down. "Stop. Stop. I'll get a charley horse."

"This little piggy had roast beef," Sioux continued as though he had gone stone deaf to her pleas.

"How about bacon? I'm hungry," she squealed.

"And this little piggy had none. And *this* little piggy went . . ." He grabbed her little toe and squeezed lightly. "What did this little piggy do?"

"He went 'wee-wee-wee' all the way home . . . and if you don't let go, that little piggy and I are definitely going to have something in common," she laughingly threatened.

"You'll never live it down if you do," he teased, letting go of her foot and ankle.

"You'd tell?" she asked in mock horror. Whipping the sheet back, she staggered to her feet and headed toward the bathroom. "Probably put it on a placard and parade up and down the

121

street!" she happily grumbled, quickly closing the door when she saw him headed toward her.

Sioux laughed aloud as he began taking the breakfast makings from the refrigerator. While she was still asleep he had mapped out a day of introducing Alex to the wonders of nature, but had almost scratched the entire day's list when she had sleepily pursed her lips to form his name. She might not be able to say the words he desperately wanted to hear, but subconsciously her mind was dwelling on him. He liked that. The other would come in time. He was a patient man; he could wait.

"Smells yummy," Alex said. She smiled at him and pinched his rump. "That's for torturing me."

Sioux graciously accepted his punishment as he used the spatula to put scrambled eggs onto her plate next to the bacon he had fried. "Ready to face the great out-of-doors?"

"You know, I'm beginning to really like this cabin," she answered, avoiding the alternative plan. "When does the tour bus arrive?"

"No bus. No sizzling pavement. No traffic. Just you and me, babe," he retorted, stoking his fork into his mouth. "You'll love it."

"False promises so early?" she teased.

"Guaranteed, money-back offer."

"You mean I'm going to have to pay?"

Sioux grinned in the villainous manner of a

used-car dealer selling a lemon. "Ma'am," he drawled, "if you aren't completely satisfied I'll double the refund as long as it's payment in kind." He glanced from Alexandria to the rumpled bed.

"Okay!" she enthusiastically agreed. "Lead away, Tonto!"

Sioux could feel his grin slipping and hid the reaction to her remark by taking another bite of bacon and eggs. She had laughingly pointed out his Indian heritage again. As he chewed he wondered if she was genuinely prejudiced? Search as he might he could not find the bitter look of contempt in her eyes. But the suspicion was as glaring as the sun reflecting off a loaded gun, and as dangerous. He'd grown up with the verbal sting of children tormenting him because he was different. The insecurities he had kept tightly controlled began breaking through their bindings. *She isn't,* he reassured himself, but the seed of doubt was subconsciously being nourished by her off-the-cuff comments.

"Grab a sack out of the second drawer, would you?" he requested. He stacked the dishes in the sink and began rinsing them.

"I'll do the dishes," she offered, beginning to feel guilty about letting Sioux do all the household chores.

"Get the sack. I'll only be a minute. You can

pack the salami, cheese, bread, and apples for a picnic lunch."

"We're going to eat outside?" she queried, inwardly grimacing.

"Haven't you ever been on a picnic? Never?" he asked incredulously when he saw her shaking her head.

"City-born; city-bred; and prefer the basic necessities of a table, chair, and napkin," she answered, confident that eating on the ground with the bugs wasn't all it was cracked up to be.

Sioux just stood there shaking his head in disbelief. *How could a grown woman have missed so much?* he wondered.

"We'll compromise. Get the quilt off the bed to use as a tablecloth," he instructed, not wanting her to feel too far out of her own element.

Hours later, as they were ambling hand in hand through the pine forest, Alex had to admit that the odor of the pines was delightful . . . far better than the artificial pine solvent she used to scrub her kitchen floor. And she liked the low tone of voice Sioux used as he pointed out various types of growth that had been used for medicinal purposes by the Indian tribe who had inhabited this part of Colorado.

As they leisurely followed a narrow path made by small animals, Sioux leading the way, she asked, "Where are we headed?"

Sioux glanced up and saw the sun shining directly overhead. "I thought we'd eat lunch down by the creek."

"Won't there be animals there getting a drink of water . . . or stalking each other?" she quizzed, knowing little of the ways of the forest but not wanting to get between the creek and a thirsty animal.

"Most forest animals feed and drink at night." Sioux grinned. "They'll be more afraid of you than you are of them."

"Humph. I doubt that," she argued. "They have sharp teeth and claws."

Sioux twisted his head and looked over his shoulder. "So do you, my dear, so do you."

A grin broke through her trepidation at being in the woods. "You ought to know," she tossed back pertly and winked.

The reward she heard, Sioux's husky laughter, went a long way toward making her day pleasant. Maybe eating on the ground wouldn't be so terrible after all, she thought, feeling decidedly adventurous. After all, she rationalized, they'd been out in the forest for hours and nothing had leaped out from behind the trees, or crawled out from beneath rocks. All in all, it was . . . enjoyable.

By the time they reached the banks of the creek, which was shaded by a blend of aspen and pines, Alex had conquered her distaste for being out of her element. Sioux was expanding her horizons and she found herself eager to learn more about living away from the city. Alex spread the quilt on the ground and sat down Indian-style. She was hungry and didn't mind showing it.

Wordlessly Sioux dropped down beside her and began unpacking the sack. Taking a knife from his pocket he whittled a chunk off the roll of salami and handed it to her with a piece of cheese.

"Starving?" he asked as he watched her gobble it down.

"Hmmmmm. I didn't know salami could taste this good," she answered, grinning appreciatively and holding out her hand for another piece.

"Want a napkin?" he teased as he saw her wiping her hand on her jeans.

"You don't have any," she retorted, slightly embarrassed by her attempt to get the residue of the salami off her hand.

"I'll bet you were the little girl who went to the birthday party and came back spic and span."

"Certainly," she agreed. "And I'll bet you were the hooligan who went around dumping ice cream on little girls' shiny patent leather shoes."

"You'd be wrong. I was the quiet child who was never invited," he admitted stonily, too proud to reveal the real reason he wasn't given an invitation.

"When's your birthday?" she asked, deciding to give him the biggest surprise party of his life.

"November twenty-sixth." Sioux raised both hands and laughed. "Don't say it. Yes, I'm a turkey."

Alex surprised him by taking a path he hadn't expected. "I was thinking how thankful your mother must have been to have had a child like you. I'll bet she still brags about her darling boy."

Sioux chuckled self-consciously—she had hit the truth—and shrugged as though he were too embarrassed to talk about it. He couldn't talk about his mother or how he felt about her without saying too much. Alex was bright, and he knew she was curious about his "secret product." Discussing his mother, the person to whom he had given his vow, would be too dangerous. He loved Alex, but he wouldn't allow himself to divulge too much.

"We'd better be heading back," he said softly when they had, in companionable silence, finished eating. "I'll have to shut up the cabin and get it ready for winter." Sioux watched the patches of sunshine glistening off Alexandria's hair and controlled the urge to wind its length around his wrist and drag her closer. A primitive side to his nature made him want to make love to her with only their isolation to protect them from prying eyes, but he didn't want to destroy the peaceful interlude with passion. He wanted her to remember the Colorado pine forests for their beauty and their beauty alone.

"Thank you for sharing your little slice of heaven," she said honestly. She rose to her feet and started folding the blanket. "I wouldn't want to live here, but it is a nice place to visit."

"Does that trite phrase mean you'd come again?" he asked as he stuffed the cellophane and other nonbiodegradable remains back into the sack.

"Sometimes trite and true are synonymous," she sparred, wishing she had thought of a more eloquent way to express what she felt.

"I like the Spanish phrase *Mi casa es su casa;* My house is your house. That, too, is trite, but it expresses how I feel. If city life gets you down, come here. Promise?"

Alex laughed aloud, and nodded her head up and down. "Of course, I'd need an Indian guide to help me find it, wouldn't I?"

"Are you accusing me of having an ulterior motive behind my generous offer?" he asked with a wicked, devilish glint in his green eyes.

It was Alex's turn to shrug.

"Could be true," he murmured. He draped his arm across her shoulders and hugged her close. "I don't think this place will ever be the same without you."

Alex placed a friendly kiss on his cheek telling him it wouldn't be the same without him, either.

* * *

Sioux gathered up the weekend's newspapers and handed them to Alexandria after she had unlocked the door to her condominium. Their loving interlude was, regretfully, on both their parts, drawing to a close.

"You don't have to rush off, do you?" Alex asked, resisting the inevitable.

"I'd like nothing more than to come in and stay, but you have some decisions you'll have to make about us before tomorrow, and much as I'd like to influence them further, it wouldn't be fair." His hand cupped the back of her neck beneath the braids she had twisted like a golden halo around her head.

"It's not my company," she explained. "Jane makes the final decisions about hiring a dubious character like you," she added in an effort to laugh about the serious topic standing between them.

The telephone shrilly began ringing from inside her home. The eyes of each of them cursed the untimely interruption. Sioux stepped inside the door and motioned for her to answer it, that he would wait.

Only one person would be calling her on a Sunday evening and she didn't want to talk to Jane while Sioux was standing there. She was torn between loyalty to her employer and this new, unnamed feeling between herself and Sioux.

"Go ahead," Sioux encouraged. "I'll wait outside." He had seen her dilemma and quickly decided to make things as easy as possible for her.

"Hello," Alex answered as she dropped the papers on the chair beside the telephone.

"Alex? Where have you been?" Jane demanded. "I've been trying to reach you since I talked to the attorney Friday. I've been worried sick. Are you okay?"

"I'm fine, Jane," Alex reassured her. "What did you find out from Sharon Stanton?"

"She wasn't too concerned until she saw the Sunday paper. Have you seen it yet?"

"It's right here, but I haven't had a chance to read it. What does the newspaper have to do with Sharon?" Alex asked, her mind refusing to connect the corporate attorney with anything in the paper.

"Don't let me destroy the effect. Open it to the front page," Jane instructed quietly.

Alexandria felt her stomach wrench with apprehension as she took off the thin sheet of plastic wrapping *The Rocky Mountain News.*

130

The two-inch headlines proclaiming intensification of the cold war with communist nations had less effect than the picture at the bottom of the page in the space reserved for human interest stories. Man and woman, herself and Sioux, clamped together in what appeared a passionate embrace with a protest placard facing the camera, telling all.

"Jane, I just walked in the door. Would you mind giving me a moment to read this and then I'll call you back?"

"Have you seen that maniac over the weekend?" Jane quizzed.

"Yes. He's here now. I'll call you right back," Alex replied, placing the phone in its cradle and slowly walking to the door.

Had the slender golden thread of trust been made of cotton twine, Alex would have been able to watch it unravel, twisting, balling up, shriveling with each step.

"Come in, Sioux. You made the front page," she commented with cool disdain as she handed the paper to him.

"Damn."

The mild expletive was the first Alex had heard him use. Was he as distressed by the public proclamation as she was? Were the lines marring his bronze face caused by stress or fatigue? His mossy-green eyes would hold the answer, but she couldn't see them. They were glued to the black print of the paper.

"Your carefully laid plan was successful," she mockingly congratulated him. "Jane must be worried or she wouldn't have been calling all weekend."

"You're damned calm about this," he said, voice raised, shaking the paper in front of her eyes. "Doesn't it bother you to have your picture plastered on the front page?"

Yes it bothers me, she wanted to scream, but didn't. Screaming and shouting wouldn't soothe the pain ripping through her chest. Her emotional roller-coaster was rushing downward at breakneck speed, but she wasn't going to let the perpetrator of the deed get any satisfaction from seeing her despair. Almost clinically she watched Sioux agitatedly pace back and forth, slapping the paper against his soft jeans.

"I can't deny having had the placard made in advance or that I had a newspaperman standing in the wings. I fought this battle with every intention of winning," he gritted between his teeth. "What I didn't plan on was becoming involved with the unknown person Alexandria Foster."

Sure you didn't, Alex thought. *Too bad you aren't on the silver screen; you'd win an Oscar.* Underneath the controlled anger Alex was silently pleading for him to tell her lies, tell her

132

anything that would absolve him from the far greater treachery of getting her out of town for the weekend, purposely, coldheartedly seducing her, making her believe he was the kind of man she could trust without reserve.

"Did you notice exactly how successful you were? UPI picked up the story. Not only will everyone in Denver sympathize with your plight, but you'll have national coverage. Don't break your arm patting yourself on your back," she icily warned. "Jane won't take this lying down." *Like I did,* she silently added.

The caustic blast halted his pacing. "You think I carted you off to the Rockies to keep you from being in touch with Jane, don't you?"

Alex answered by raising her eyebrow. Inside her mind she begged him to deny the facts. She wanted to believe in his innocence, but the facts were damning.

"You're letting past experience prejudice your viewpoint. I'm not deceitful or sneaky. You know that, don't you?" he stated firmly.

When he saw the defiant sparks, icicle daggers, being shot at him, he knew the friendship, the trust, he had diligently worked toward building one fragile block at a time were crumbling before his eyes, and there was no way of stopping it. The pain lurking in the depths of her golden eyes was evident. He took a step forward, desiring to comfort the pain away, but halted when she pivoted away from him.

"Thank you for an educational weekend," she murmured. "I'd appreciate it if you'd leave. Jane is waiting for my call."

Sioux's mind raced in an effort to right the wrong, heal the wound gaping in his chest. What could he say? Yes, he had determinedly pursued his goal of being hired by Beautiful Cosmetics. Yes, he had considered any means justifiable. Yes, he had known about the picture.

"Why did you agree to go with me?" he asked, wanting her to remember the feeling of having found the other half of her soul.

Alex didn't want to remember her foolish behavior. She denied him the response she knew he wanted to hear by saying, "Jane told me to distract you until she had contacted our attorney."

Swirling around, she had the satisfaction of seeing Sioux blanch, as though he'd been cut to the very heart. Why was her mouth acidic instead of sweet with the taste of a minor victory? It was true; Jane had told her to divert him; she had followed orders . . . more or less. *Far more than less,* she ruefully admitted, but only to herself.

"That's not true," he negated firmly. "You wouldn't prostitute yourself to protect Jane. You care for me, Alexandria. Tell me you lied," he quietly ordered, opening his arms toward her. "Tell the truth; it will be worth it in the long run."

She gave an unnatural, high-pitched laugh. "You've got to be kidding. Gut level you know the truth. You know of my loyalty to Jane and the company. You know I've never hired a man. You don't think you're the first to apply, do you?" she scoffed, praying she could blink back the tears which threatened to slide from the corners of her eyes. "Women can be every bit as ruthless as men." *Other women, not me*, she realized acutely, feeling as though every bone in her body had splintered and was painfully slicing into each of her vital organs.

"I don't believe you, Alexandria. You're hurt by what you see as another betrayal by a man. When you've calmed down, when this mess is cleared up, you'll realize just how much I care." Sioux's hands opened. The paper fell to the floor between them with a thud. Resigned, he crossed to the door. As he felt the cold brass knob in the palm of his hand he knew he couldn't leave without telling her what was inscribed on his soul. Slowly turning, openly making himself vulnerable to scorn, he murmured softly, "I love you, Alexandria Foster. You can trust me."

CHAPTER EIGHT

Alex wasn't about to let a smooth lie stand between her and her duty to Jane. Those three words were too easily said by the man who had deliberately set about to break the "no men" policy at Beautiful Cosmetics. Jane had decided to play a waiting game and Sioux had laid siege to the fort manned by women. For two weeks Alex refused to go anywhere near the window in her office. She knew he was there, pacing from one end of the building to the other, carrying the same damned placard.

The first few days Martha had listened to the gossip being carried around the production line and had gleefully reported back to her boss what was being said. There wasn't a woman working at Beautiful Cosmetics who wouldn't

136

have given her cosmetics discount to be photographed with Sioux. His name was on everyone's lips except Alexandria's.

She fielded the numerous phone calls from the press, from other male applicants who wanted to jump on the publicity bandwagon, from the attorney, but refused the daily noon call from Sioux. At first she had expected him to storm the portals and demand to see her, but he didn't. Not once did he enter the double swinging doors of Beautiful Cosmetics. It was as though a peace bond restricted him to the outside pavement. To avoid his piercing eyes each morning she had parked her car on the back lot rather than the reserved space in front.

Only at night did she allow her heart the solace of remembering a better time, a better place. Her nerves frayed from the constant demands of the working day, she would utterly collapse when she arrived home. Although she could put her emotional involvement on the back burner when at work, she couldn't in her own home. She relived each moment they had shared, dissecting, adding, deleting, revising their conversations. Long into the night she mulled through the cause and effects of how she felt about Sioux the Schemer. Her heart, uninhibited by her mental damper, reminded her of the protective way he had held her when she was scared. It reminded her of why he had left

137

the pharmaceutical industry. It reminded her, most painfully, of the tears she had shed for him. But the cerebral Virgo dismissed those factors as irrelevant . . . all part of his scheming, deceiving plot to undermine her decision not to hire him.

Jane entered her office, shoulders bent instead of regally erect, and heaved a heavy sigh as she fell prostrate on Alex's sofa.

"It's over. I fought like hell, but we lost. The Office of Economic Opportunity called. They're being pressured by public opinion to file against us. We have to hire him or face a costly court battle. What do you think?"

Alex watched as Jane crossed her ankles and folded her arms over her forehead. Defeat was a bitter pill for her mentor to swallow. She'd won a thousand victories, but Sioux had ambushed her with hit-and-run tactics she couldn't defend herself against. The law was the law was the law, she silently read on Jane's face. Hiring women who had been refused jobs because of their sex wasn't a valid argument in the courtroom. Having women at the helm of a thriving industry was a personal insult against every man who was struggling to keep his business afloat. The very people who had praised the shining example of feminine competence were now swaying the pendulum toward the opposite pole. They condemned as glibly as they had praised.

"We could hire him and stick him in a closet to ferment," Alex suggested in an attempt to bring a smile to Jane's distraught face. "Or better yet, we could build an outhouse on the far end of the parking lot and issue him only explosive chemicals to test."

Jane snorted. "Do you remember him promising a 'miracle product'?" she asked, swinging her feet to the plush carpet. "I want all rights." Raising her hands to halt Alex's interruption, she continued, "I know. It wasn't developed here, and I can't demand the patent legally, but, dammit, the man has had it all go his way. I want exclusive rights to anything he has invented!"

"I'll do whatever you want, but really, Jane, you didn't believe the carrot he dangled in front of us, did you? His secret product is probably a squeeze tube of Preparation H."

"I feel as though I could use it. Sioux Compton has been a genuine pain in my posterior. Passing a brick would be easier for me to do than hiring a man to fill a vacancy," Jane admitted. "You never did find a competent replacement other than Sioux, did you?"

Alex shook her head. She'd scarcely had time to rob a chemist from another company and shelter Jane from the outside forces which had constantly battered at the door.

"It doesn't matter. I'll go down and wave the white flag. You negotiate the terms of surrender.

Quite frankly I don't have the stomach for it."
Jane rubbed her hand above her trim waistline
as though she had recently developed an ulcer.
"We'll have to arrange a media conference in
the immediate future. Maybe we'll tag on a plug
for one of the new Christmas fragrances," she
mused, always attuned to the slightest angle.
"We might as well get some good press out of
this for a change."

Staring down at her desktop, blinking back
the salty tears of sorrow for her mentor's defeat,
she resolved to negotiate a no-loophole contract
that would make Sioux squirm beneath his war
bonnet.

Firm in her resolution, she clamped her pen
in her hand and began jotting down notes.
Sharon would have to go over them to make
certain they were legal, but she needed a general outline to work from. Sioux's being in the
same room would have emotional impact and
she didn't want to be distracted by those doubts
her heart constantly bubbled to the surface of
her dreams.

Too soon Martha announced the arrival of *Mr.*
Sioux Compton. Alex leaned back in her swivel
chair in an effort to give the image of being in
complete control. She wouldn't extend the
courtesy she showed other people who entered
her office by rising to her feet. *Let him think*

we're negotiating from strength rather than weakness.

"Alexandria," Sioux greeted in his low voice as he entered her domain.

"Mr. Compton," she formalized, "be seated."

"Jane said you wanted to see me," he croaked, then cleared his throat. *Let it be the man, not the prospective employee she wants to see,* he fervently prayed. *Let the woman speak, not the robot extension of Lady Jane.*

"We've decided to review your application, Mr. Compton. However, should we decide to employ you, there will be certain stipulations." Alex let her voice drone at a businesslike rate. To her own ears she sounded like a tape recording of a correspondence course in business administration. "You mentioned a . . . product. What is it?"

"I'm not at liberty to discuss the product until we've come to some mutually agreeable terms, Alexandria," he answered dispassionately. His prayers had been denied. R2D2 from *Star Wars* had more inflection and warmth in his blippity-blips than she did.

"We'll hire you . . . if you relinquish all rights to your mysterious product," she coolly informed him. She'd kept her eyes focused inches above his head, but when she felt the tautness of her nerves easing, she lowered them to level with his eyes.

It was a mistake. The yearning was clearly evident behind the frozen mask, which was more deeply tanned than she remembered. His eyes were flowing over her features one by one as though he were a starving man presented with a mile-long buffet table laden with gourmet delicacies. They dwelled on her lips, the fine silver necklace circling her slender neck, and slowly, hesitantly, fell to the V of her beige blouse. He was visually devouring her.

"Mr. Compton, I'd appreciate having your entire attention," she reprimanded in what she was certain was a bold cover-up for the quivering mass of Jell-O to which he had reduced her insides.

Sioux, using the back of his hand, wiped away the thin film of perspiration from his forehead. *I'm probably sending smoke signals from my ears.* He knew by heart the message they would transmit: *I love you, Alexandria Foster.*

"You have it," he murmured barely above a whisper. "I've missed you, Alexandria. Have you missed me?" His need to hear anything from her lips other than words revolving around business was acutely essential.

"How could I miss you? You've been here every day . . . right under my feet," she curtly replied as she pointed to her window.

"Did you watch me? I've counted every window from left to right as I tried to remember where yours would be," he admitted.

"Sioux . . . dredging up old memories is painful. Let's be kind to each other and communicate on a less personal basis."

The catch in her voice burst any illusion she projected of being hardhearted. Had she been able to talk to him without doubting the concreteness of her own conclusions, she could have carried off the corporate-woman image. But when the longing was openly displayed on his face, when the torment was there for her clearly to see, she did wonder if she had been blind. Had he been telling the truth all along? Had he meant it, truly meant it, when he said he loved her? When he accused her of viewing mankind through experience-distorted lenses, had he been right? Was she letting pain inflicted on an immature eighteen-year-old narrow her eyesight . . . allowing only dark tunnel-vision?

"Alexandria, have you ever seen an animal when it's wounded? A dog struck by a car? Do you know what happens when someone stops to try and help it? It snarls. It growls. It snaps at the person who wants to minister to its pain." Sioux stopped. More to himself than to Alex he whispered, "I don't know which of us is feeling worse." He propped his elbow on her desk, leaned forward, and cupped the side of his head in his hand. "If you're hurting, let me be the one to help you. If I'm the only one hurting, for God's sake, take me home with you and put me out of my misery."

"I can't trust you not to bite," she replied, her lips curving into the first beginnings of a smile.

"Don't tease me now, please. I didn't know for certain the picture would be in the paper. I didn't drag you out to the boonies to keep you from communicating with Jane. I swear I didn't. You have to trust me, Alexandria."

"Trust? I'm not certain I'm capable of trusting you or any other man," she honestly admitted. "I wanted to trust you. I've asked myself a million times why I didn't say, 'Sioux, I trust you. Explain why you picketed Beautiful Cosmetics and literally forced us to employ you when obviously, you could have gotten a job anywhere. Tell me what this wonderful discovery is that you've made.' Can you answer those questions? Make me trust you. Prove you're worthy of trusting."

Sioux's head dropped; his hands strung through his dark hair were the only things keeping his face from smashing into the desktop. "I can't answer those questions," he mumbled. "Not because I don't want to. I do. It isn't my secret to divulge. I swore I wouldn't."

Both of Alex's palms struck the desktop forcefully. "Forget trust! Let's get down to business."

"It won't be long until you have all the an-

144

swers," he promised, regretting the rigid boundaries of his integrity. He'd have to wait. Be patient. When Alexandria learned, firsthand, that he had every intention of making Beautiful Cosmetics the byword whispered on the lips of half the population, male and female, she would understand. He had to believe that or completely lose touch with reality and grovel at her feet.

"I can't haggle with you over details," he said, raising his head, turning toward the window, giving Alexandria only the side view of his noble profile. "I'll have my attorney contact you."

"In that case our business is finished, Mr. Compton. I hope you enjoy all you've worked so hard to gain." Her tone was bitterly unrefinedly sarcastic.

The true message was shouting, reverberating off the walls: We're finished. Enjoy your Pyrrhic victory.

"I won't give up, Alexandria. What I've done isn't morally wrong." Slowly rising to his feet, he knew how a whipped dog felt. He also knew he'd be leaving the room with his tail between his legs unless he straightened up. Pride and his age-old heritage came to his rescue. A stoic peace entered his bloodstream as he reminded himself: *What I'm doing is right.*

* * *

145

Sioux held fast to his dream. He steadily refused to give the patent rights to Jane's attorney. In the end, five nerve-wracking days later, he signed a contract which allowed him to work independently in Beautiful Cosmetics' computerized laboratory, and keep fifty percent of the profits on this product and all others he might develop, but there was a deadline for perfection of his product. He had two weeks to produce it or he would voluntarily resign.

Amid an array of ingredients provided by the corporation, and by himself, he worked day and night. Tired, bleary eyed, two days prior to the ax falling, he was still testing and retesting, testing and retesting. A small vial of flesh-colored liquid was the end product. Sioux laid his head to rest on the countertop. He knew Jane and Alex would laugh when they first saw it. He could almost hear them saying, "A base foundation? *That was the big secret?*" As he drifted into sleep a smile hovered on his lips.

"It was worth it," he mumbled, giving way to the sleepy demands of his body.

* * *

While Sioux was sleeping, Jane was gloating to Alex.

"November twenty-fourth is just around the corner. The enemy in our camp will peacefully withdraw, and everything will be normal

146

around here again. I've arranged a news conference. He can either demonstrate his 'miracle product' or humbly resign." Jane rubbed her hands together in anticipation of the latter eventuality.

"Have you found out anything?" Alex asked, suddenly concerned for Sioux's health. "No one has seen him for days."

"Well," Jane replied drily, "if he died we'd have begun to smell him by now." She chuckled at the pleasant thought. "You aren't worried about him after what he did to you, are you?"

Alex had given Jane a scanty picture of how she and Sioux had spent the weekend at his cabin, and Jane had guessed the rest. If he failed, Alex knew, Jane would be professionally vindicated, and thought she would be personally vindicated.

"He is an employee," Alex reminded her, "and entitled to the concern we would have for any employee who was working himself to death."

"Pshaw! He isn't entitled to anything. He had his reward in advance."

Alex flushed. "I almost hope he makes it." She sighed. "It's irrational, but I do."

"He'll be a rich man if he does. How do you feel about rich men?" Jane probed as she pulled her glasses out of her pocket and perched them on her nose as though doing so would give her greater insight into Alex's behavior.

"Somehow I don't think money is important to Sioux. Honor. Trust. Maybe love. But not money."

"You're in love with him, aren't you?" Jane demanded, a bit awestruck by Alex's character analysis of Sioux. "Love is blinding you to his faults, my dear. The flaws are there. They are real, not imagined."

"I've done a whole vatful of thinking, Jane, and the reason he refused to budge was he'd given his word to someone. Probably someone he is duty-bound to, as I am to you."

Jane removed her glasses, indicating she didn't want to see or hear any more. Dependence in their case was a two-way street. Loyalty and friendship were a shared commodity and Jane didn't want to overweight the balance.

"It's early afternoon. Why don't you take the man a sandwich? Use it as an excuse to check on him. If he's sleeping on the job, willing to admit defeat, tell him we'll go easy on him."

"Benign dictatorship?" Alex teased.

"You always could get around me if you tried. Go on, Alex. Get your own head screwed on straight. To misquote a famous gentleman, 'Frankly, my dear, you look like hell!'"

"Thanks," Alex drawled as she pulled a mirror out of her desk drawer. She knew she looked like the "before" in a before-and-after picture. Tiny wrinkles were becoming permanent from the perpetual scowl on her face. The hair she had prided herself in lacked luster. Alex grimaced when she glanced at her fingernails. They were chewed off to the quick.

Jane shrugged. "You know we insist on everyone from myself to the ladies filling the boxes looking her best. It's part of the glamor industry."

"I know." Alex sighed. "But I've had a bad case of the doldrums lately."

"You're not pregnant, are you?" Jane blurted out before she could rephrase the question more delicately.

"No. I said doldrums, not dumb-dumbs."

"Time cures all, my dear. Maybe you need a paid vacation to gay Paree."

"Sometime next year when I've cleared off this pile"—her hand thumped the stack of papers on the "in" tray—"I'll consider it." Alex watched as the older woman gracefully rose to her alligator-clad feet and headed toward the door. "Jane . . . thanks. It's good to know someone cares."

Jane grinned, waved nonchalantly, and proceeded through the door.

The mirror hung limply from Alex's fingers. Jane's question had made her face a fact she had consciously avoided. Alexandria Foster loves

149

Sioux Compton. The need to do something constructive, other than sift through the facts like a miner searching for gold, was suddenly driving her. She couldn't face Sioux resembling a newspaper wrapping a dead fish, she decided. The best she could do in her office was to braid her hair, put on some fresh makeup, and valiantly go forth into battle.

Alexandria peeped between the miniblinds, peering through the thick plate-glass window before opening his locked door with her key. A grin slashed her lips. Sioux was sacked out. Wouldn't Jane get her jollies if she could see him now? she mused. Quietly she closed the door and twisted the plastic rod which shut the miniblinds.

There was something . . . touching about watching Sioux completely relaxed. His dark lashes, long and curling, made half-moon shadows on his high cheekbones. Instead of a cocky dimpled smile she was used to seeing, his lips were sensuously full, slightly parted. The unruly dark hair looked as though he had repeatedly drawn his fingers from his temple to the crown of his head, which left it wildly tousled.

A tight band of love circled her heart, making it thump loudly in the silence of the laboratory. He's beautiful, she thought, her throat constricting. It was silly, but she was experiencing the same emotion Sioux had talked about when he saw something pure in its beauty. Tears, ones usually shed when in pain, were gathering on her lower lids. Wiping the foolish tears away with the back of her hand, she sniffed loudly.

Sioux opened one eye a fraction of an inch. *What is Alexandria doing here?* he sleepily wondered. *Maybe she isn't here at all. Maybe she's a hallucination. Maybe I've finally crossed the brink of insanity.*

"Alexandria?" he called, voice slurred from drowsiness. Startled, she jumped as though he had stung her. "Whaterya doin' here?" he asked. His tongue was slow, dry, sticking to the roof of his mouth.

"Hunting for Diogenes," she glibly replied, moving to within arm's reach of him.

"Out of stock," he mumbled, blinking his eyes to make certain she wasn't a figment of his imagination.

"How about lit lanterns?" she throatily asked, unable to resist the temptation to run her hand over the rumpled lab jacket stretched across his shoulders.

"Could we start this conversation over? My brain is on malfunction and nothing seems to be sinking in."

Sioux straightened, circling her slender waist with one arm and pulling her closer. The combined floral bouquet fragrance filled his senses as he turned on his high stool and buried his face

151

in the crook of her neck and shoulder. His other arm wrapped lazily around her hips as he spread his thighs apart and drew her closer.

"You're being awfully familiar during working hours," she lightly reprimanded him, chuckling with glee as she clung to his shoulders.

"What's Diogenes?" he mumbled between light kisses across her collarbone.

"Not what . . . who. A man who carries a lantern throughout eternity searching for an honest man," she softly explained, fingering the short dark hair above his ear. "I think, maybe, he needs to stop in at Beautiful Cosmetics."

Alexandria could feel his lips curving into a smile and the kisses rising up her neck, pausing at the pulsebeat, then spreading over her jawline toward the uptilted curve of her own mouth. Against her lips he asked, "What makes you think his search would end here?"

"You."

Ever so gently, ever so sweetly, Sioux prevented any further explanation by closing his mouth over hers. He didn't need more, not for the moment. It was enough that she was here, in his arms, believing in his honesty.

"It's soup," he whispered, lightly puffing the last sound against her cheek.

"What's soup?" Alexandria asked dreamily, raining tiny pecks on the arch of his dark eyebrow.

He answered with another question. "Haven't you seen the commercial where the kid yells, 'Is it soup yet?' "

Nodding her head affirmatively, she wondered if his sealed-lip kiss had shorted out her electricity, making her mind unable to decode any message he was sending.

"The 'big-secret' product is ready for final testing." He grinned, proud that he could finally clear up all the misunderstandings. "Wanna see?"

"Mmmmmmm. Not now," she whispered, using the pads of her fingers to outline the curve of his ear.

Sioux laughed, full of joy. After one quick nuzzle against her breasts he separated himself from her by holding her upper arms, standing, and taking a step backward. Alexandria couldn't help but notice the green sparkle in his eyes. He was like a kid with a new toy that he wanted to show to his favorite friend.

The vial was lying on its side where it had fallen out of his hand while he slept. "That's it," Sioux proudly proclaimed as he placed it in Alexandria's hand.

"That's what?"

"A new base coat," he answered, making his voice mysterious.

"Terrific. Just what we need," Alexandria said, injecting as much enthusiasm as she could. They had a complete line of base coats. He would have been better off sticking to hand cream, she thought wryly.

"You don't sound pleased," he commented, a chuckle building in his chest. "Instead of having to mix six or seven different colors, this one will complement any skin color."

"Oh, yeah?" Alex said as she unscrewed the top and squeezed a small amount on the back of her hand and rubbed it in.

It blended in with her own skin tones beautifully. Not completely satisfied, she took Sioux's hand, squeezed again, and watched as it magically changed colors to blend with his darker coloring.

"That's fantastic!" she enthused with sincerity. "Have you any idea how much production cost we can cut by being able to mix one batch?"

"That's not all." Sioux pulled out a drawer and extracted two snapshots. He showed first one, then the other. "See any difference?"

Bending down, Alexandria switched her honey-colored eyes from one photograph to the other. "Are you telling me this is the same woman in both pictures?"

"Um-hmmm." His finger traced over the brow of the woman in the first picture, which was deeply lined. "Notice the age wrinkles and sun wrinkles on her cheeks and throat." Pointing to the other picture he asked, "See any here?"

"No," she marveled. "They're gone. Face-lift?" she asked, unable to believe what she was seeing.

"Nope. Beautiful Cosmetics' new base coat!" He grabbed her and swung her around and around.

Laughing, kissing, dizzy from being swung around, Alexandria gasped, saying, "Put me down. We'll go get Jane, show her the new product, then let her take us out to lunch for a champagne celebration!"

The mention of Alexandria's mentor's name took the wind out of his sails. The second person to know about his success was *not* going to be Lady Jane. Taking Alex's hand, he pulled her behind him through the door, making a sharp left, heading toward the production room.

"She's in her office," Alex protested, starting to drag her heels.

"Not the lady we're going to see. The woman responsible for my being here," he countered, and gave her restraining arm a sharp tug.

Bewildered, Alexandria tagged along like a puppy on a leash. On a euphoric high, she didn't really care where Sioux took her as long as they were together. Smiling, radiant, she murmured brief hellos to the women they passed.

They reached the stainless steel table where

two women, one dark skinned, the other fair, sat checking the packaging on a special fragrance designed for the Christmas market. Alex would have known which woman Sioux wanted to see by the expression on the older woman's face, and the perfect smoothness of the cheeks and brow of the woman she'd seen in the picture.

Standing aside, she watched Sioux cross to both women, raising his voice to be heard over the automatic packaging machine which was with precise regularity accepting the bottle, folding the flaps, and setting it upright for inspection.

"Mother, can you get away for a moment?" Sioux asked.

Mother? Sioux's mother is one of our employees? Pieces of the puzzle began falling into place as, dumbfounded, she watched mother and son moving toward her, an identical smile with matching dimples creasing both of their faces. Alexandria knew this woman. She'd worked for Beautiful Cosmetics for years.

Sioux cupped the elbows of his mother and Alexandria and led them toward a quieter area. "Alexandria, I want you to meet the woman responsible for my being here—my mother."

The beaming pride of the short woman as she gazed from her son toward Alexandria was unmistakable. Almost timidly she offered her hand in greeting.

"You won't fire me now, will you?" Mrs. Compton asked, her brown eyes expressing worry.

Alexandria hugged the woman in response. "Fire you? You've got to be kidding! Your son has invented the most fantastic product imaginable! We may make you vice-president in charge of production."

"I did produce a fine man, didn't I?" she replied, including Sioux, making it a three-way hug.

"Mother, I know you have to get back, but I wanted you to know that, thanks to the computer in the lab, I've worked out the kinks in the formula." Sioux laughed. "It won't be long before you can tell everyone the name of your plastic surgeon."

"Thank goodness." She chuckled with a mock sigh of relief. "I have to get back. Rumor is the boss lady is in the plant." She kissed Alexandria's cheek and twitted, "I've heard she's intolerant of people who conduct personal business on company time." Kissing her son's stubbly chin, she whispered, "You can tell her," and proudly walked back to her stool.

"She's the one you gave the promise to, isn't she?" Alexandria asked, finally comprehending why Sioux had flatly refused to break his oath. "She was afraid of losing her job if we found out you were her son."

157

Sioux nodded and then draped his arm around her waist and guided her back toward the office section of the building. The steady hum of machines filling plastic tubes, bottom first, crimpling the end, and ejecting the filled container into a cardboard box made conversation difficult. Alex knew the women in the factory would be eager for their break time to speculate on the meaning of the scene: Alexandria, right-hand woman of Lady Jane, consorting with . . . an employee, a man, Sioux Compton, chief chemist.

CHAPTER NINE

"Do you want to drop the bomb, or shall I?" Alexandria asked, unable to mask the excitement in her voice.

"We'll do it together," he answered gruffly, lightly shoving her into the confines of his lab, closing and relocking the door. "We're going to be doing everything . . . together," he growled in triumph when he had stalked her backward until she was pressed against the back wall. "Aren't we?"

"For a man who was exhausted, you've certainly made a swift recovery."

"Your kisses are the magic ingredient," he rasped, dipping down to refresh himself with her sweetness.

His hands, one on either side of her head, slid

up the surface of the white wall as he pressed closer. The effect she had on him was instantaneous. Sioux was unable to control the tightening below his belt any more than he could keep the low groan in the back of his throat when Alexandria cupped his buttocks and erotically swayed her hips against him.

"Do I hear a dog barking?" Alexandria lightly teased. She grinned when Sioux raised his head, cocking it to one side. "Remember the dog who was in pain who growls and snaps?"

"Ummm-hmmm," he hummed against her lips. "Me. I'm definitely in pain. I promise not to bite if you take me home and patch me up."

"Won't it be awkward making love with your . . . bandages?" Alex joked, loving the feel of having him intimately pressed against her breasts, her thighs, and the source of her own achey pain.

"I'll improvise. Right now I'm figuring out a way to make love to you here, now. You once told me 'anywhere, anytime, any way.' Would you make love to me here?" he rasped, his breathing rate keeping pace with the acceleration of his heartbeat.

The muscles under her hands bunched as his masculine shaft probed against the softness of her stomach. "How?"

With the mischievousness of randy teen-agers they began listing the unlikely places they could make love, and lovingly rejected each one as either physically impossible or drastically uncomfortable. Their kisses became more intoxicating than any chemical potion. They caressed each other frenziedly as they realized that the possibility of consummating their desire was thwarted by their location.

"Enough," Sioux insisted with a groan when Alexandria suggested clearing off a countertop. "You'll just have to control your raging lust," he muttered to himself.

Ducking beneath his braced arms, Alexandria straightened her blouse, and twisted her plaid woolen skirt around until the zipper was back on the side rather than half open in front. "You're a wicked, wicked man, Sioux Compton." She giggled.

"And you love wicked men, don't you?"

She caught the serious question lurking beneath his teasing one and inwardly smiled. There were no longer any doubts about trustworthiness or honorability between them. Her heart sang as she solemnly replied, "I love you."

His back to the wall, Sioux sagged, bending at the waist, sliding downward until his rear end rested on his heels. Slowly he raised his head, his eyes glowing as they followed their natural ascent from her ankles upward. "You aren't fooling around, are you?"

"No," she answered, twisting his words, "but I'd like to."

"You pick the damndest times to joke," he said with a grunt. "I never know if you're kidding or serious."

"Get off the floor. Take my hand," she coaxed softly.

Sioux entwined their fingers and used his legs to push himself upward. Alex knew she wasn't strong enough to pull him off the floor; she also knew he would always stand on his own feet . . . proudly.

"I love you," she declared without a smile, serious as a judge in long, black robes.

"Enough to marry me?" Sioux asked, hoping he wasn't pressing too hard, too fast.

"More than enough."

"And trust?" Love wasn't enough. The scars from her first marriage had to be eliminated, also.

"Implicitly," she promised.

Alexandria wasn't certain, but she thought she saw a trace of moisture behind the fringes of his eyelashes before he closed his eyes and enfolded her in the warmth of his arms. They rocked back and forth, mutually understanding how the other felt. They were one, soulmates in the finest sense of the word, Alexandria thought.

"Shall we go tell Jane?" Sioux huskily asked.

"I'd like that," Alexandria replied serenely.

How had he known Jane would be the one she'd want to know first? Somehow he knew Jane was her surrogate mother and deserved the privilege of being the first to be told of their upcoming marriage. "Can I ask her to be a bridesmaid?"

Sioux chuckled. "Something tells me Lady Jane would rather go barefoot across hot coals than walk down the aisle at a wedding."

Hooking her arm through his, Alexandria joined his infectious laughter. She was proud of the man beside her. The red, blue, green, and white squares of the Rubik's Cube were lining up. Each square contained its own secret. It wasn't necessary for Alex to answer the questions which had made her distrust Sioux to begin with. The placard with her name lettered on it was no longer a mystery. Mrs. Compton, once again via the grapevine, would have been able to tell her son about the all-woman hiring policy. The only way he could have been hired by Beautiful Cosmetics would have been by applying public pressure. Nothing less than notoriety would have broken the unwritten code. She wondered why he hadn't taken his product and sold it to a New York–based cosmetics manufacturer, but decided to be thankful he hadn't. With this base coat Beautiful Cosmetics would soon be outdoing the sales of all the other companies combined.

"Jane, we have wonderful news," Alexandria bubbled as she preceded Sioux into the president's office.

"You're getting married," Jane stated flatly. "Am I about to lose my right arm or can we Indian-wrestle for her?"

"Jane! What happened to the woman who despised people who make sly, prejudicial innuendos? Why, you said you'd fire me if you even suspected prejudice!" Confused by Jane's change in attitude, embarrassed for Sioux, she blasted the woman as she never had before.

Sioux wasn't surprised by Jane's resistance to the possibility of being replaced by a man, any man, but he was jolted into happy delirium when he realized his fears of Alexandria's being the slightest bit prejudiced were unfounded. He could have walked around Jane's desk and hugged the woman.

Jane eyed Sioux shrewdly. She had suspected Sioux's fear; he had too much pride in his heritage to ignore Alex's barbed remarks, which Jane realized were based on her bad experience with men in general. Better to bring it out in the open prior to the marriage than let Sioux smolder and misunderstand, which would lead them down a miserable marital road.

Alexandria watched as Sioux moved a straight-backed chair directly in front of Jane's desk, sat down, and assumed the pose of an arm wrestler.

"Don't be ridiculous," Alex protested. "I'm not some saloon girl of a hundred years ago. I won't be the prize of a ridiculous contest!"

Their elbows on the desk, palms together, Sioux advised in a low, amused voice, "Ms. Alex, a.k.a. Alexandria, stay out of things you don't understand."

"Don't understand! You're acting like a couple of fools . . . both of you." She directed a fiery glance at both implacably straight faces.

"Sit down and shut up," Lady Jane ordered. "You might learn something."

Alexandria had never in her life stomped her foot in rage, but she came close to it as she flounced down in a chair at the side of the desk.

The battle began in earnest. Sioux, mercifully, didn't down the woman's arm with one swift thrust as he easily could have. He appeared content to keep their arms in a perpendicular position.

"I'll resign immediately if this lunacy doesn't stop," Alex threatened quietly.

Jane ignored the threat, concentrating on applying pressure to Sioux's hand and arm.

"I won't marry you," she huffed in Sioux's direction.

"Don't distract me," Sioux answered softly.

"If the back of my hand touches the desktop I won't be marrying you."

Appalled by both of them, mentor and lover, resorting to physical force, she slumped back in her chair and glared.

Sioux locked eyes as well as hands with Lady Jane. Physically he could dominate this woman. They both knew it. The steely determination of his opponent matched his own.

"Alexandria's marrying me doesn't mean your right arm will be amputated," he began persuading.

"She survived one marital disaster; you could destroy her." Jane gritted her teeth, applying more pressure with her forearm.

"You have my word, Lady Jane. I'll cherish and protect Alexandria. I love her," he coaxed, his arm remaining upright.

"The grapevine says you've perfected your discovery. Have you?" Jane countered, relaxing the pressure.

"Yes," Sioux answered, loosening his grip on her palm. "Beautiful Cosmetics has a one-color base coat which not only covers, but delays, the aging process."

"Money?" she grunted.

"The biggest share will be spent on funding scholarships . . . for minority groups and women." A grin Sioux could no longer restrain slashed his face and he added with devilish delight, "The balance will be spent feathering a nest for your prospective grandchildren." Sioux straightened his fingers.

Alexandria's anger dissipated faster than morning dew under a burning sun. There was little doubt in her mind she had misread the encounter. Neither of them was pressing for a win. Sioux had risked everything by giving his worthy opponent an open opportunity to slam his arm into the desk. Cued by the victorious sparks shooting between their eyes, they mutually turned their hands into the recognized handshake grip of friends.

"Learn anything?" Jane asked Alex as she merrily winked at Sioux, keeping a firm grip on his hand.

"Yeah. How long I can hold my breath without croaking. The next time you two . . . *chiefs* lock horns I'm going to do the civilized thing and bean both of you with something that will split your inch-thick skulls!"

Jane and Sioux laughed at her empty warning. The volume increased when Alexandria reached over and placed her hand over both of theirs, thinking the three of them, working together, were an unbeatable team.

"Two items left on the agenda," Lady Jane stated, returning to her familiar role as chief administrator. "One, I want to see this concoction; two, we'll announce Sioux's hiring at the

167

television press conference and demonstrate the new product. Any objections?"

"None," both Alexandria and Sioux replied in unison.

"Might as well make some money while we're clearing our hiring-practice record. Just out of curiosity, Sioux, why Beautiful Cosmetics? If the product is what you claim, you could have sold it to any glamor house."

"You hired my mother when no one else would. It was Beautiful Cosmetics' weekly salary that kept food on our table and a roof over our heads. This pays off the debt . . . handsomely," Sioux explained.

"Inside informant," Jane mused aloud. "I was too arrogant to consider one of my people being behind your plot. Good thing. You know what I'd have done had I discovered the setup, don't you?"

"Mother swore me to secrecy." His eyes drifted toward Alexandria. "There were times when I was tempted to break that promise."

Alexandria knew exactly where and when she had tested his basic integrity. Each of them had strong loyalty ties to another that placed them in direct conflict. Her golden eyes swept over his dark hair and sharp features, admiring the inner beauty of a man she could, without reservations, trust.

Lady Jane nodded as she comprehended the

thin line Sioux had walked. "You might as well know, I'm not changing my policy about hiring men . . . merely making you the exception that proves the rule. Women will always have an edge at Beautiful Cosmetics."

Sioux chuckled. "I tried to convince Mother to accept the formula and present it, but unfortunately I needed the use of your computers to work out some bugs."

"Are they worked out now?" Lady Jane inquired.

"I wasn't certain the term hypoallergenic could be used in advertising. There are elements which some women will be allergic to," he answered truthfully. "But I've worked out the other problems."

"Between thee and me, we both know there are women who are allergic to putting anything on their faces . . . including pure water," Jane scoffed. "Alex, I want you to make the statement to the press about hiring Sioux, and I want you to wear the makeup."

"Me!" she exclaimed. "The public wants to see you. You're the Lady behind Beautiful Cosmetics," she protested.

"Not this time. How can I claim a miracle product when I'm a mass of fine-line wrinkles? I'll be a prime candidate for advertisement later . . . but not in two days."

"I don't know," Alex murmured hesitantly.

169

"Public speaking isn't my forte. I'm strictly a behind-the-scenes woman."

"This isn't a request; it's an order," Jane briskly informed her. Eyes shifting to Sioux, she tacked on, "Alex has been spoon-feeding words into my mouth for years. It will be refreshing to see how she wraps her mouth around some of those tongue-twisting phrases."

The odds for changing Lady Jane's mind are zero and none, Alexandria thought as she gracefully rose to her feet. What the lady couldn't and wouldn't understand was her absolute paralysis when speaking in front of more than three people. She knew her knees would be knocking faster than a Spanish dancer's castanets.

"You'll do fine," Sioux assured her. After a final handshake with his employer, Sioux cupped Alex's elbow and escorted her out the door. The twisted lips and frightened eyes told him she was scared spitless. "We'll work on it together."

The short distance to her office was covered in silence. Alexandria didn't notice the broad grin on Martha's face, or see her reaching for the telephone to spread the latest word, as she stiffly marched through her door. Sioux led her to the sofa and watched her with the same rigidity sit down. She looked as though her joints had developed a severe case of rust.

"You are scared to death, aren't you?" he asked softly as he sat closely beside her.

Speechless, she nodded her head up and down, her brow pleated in consternation.

"Remember how scared you were at the cabin? Bears lurking in corners, creepy-crawlies scuttering beneath your feet, monstrous pythons winding around the limbs of trees?"

"Yes." She hiccuped.

"Who protected you from those imaginary demons?" Sioux brushed her hair back from her face, pushing it tenderly behind her ears. "The old Indian dragon-slayer, right?"

"This is a different kind of jungle, but a jungle nonetheless. Those television cables get wrapped around my feet. Their camera has a big, red eye that focuses in on you like a space monster. And the person who interviews you is the killer. The questions he asks are deadly," she whispered, barely able to voice her fears.

Sioux wrapped his arm around her and pulled her onto his lap. With soothing, gentle, soft hands he rubbed up and down her ramrod-straight spine until he felt her begin to relax and cuddle against him, resting her chin against the curve of his neck.

"Didn't I protect you over the weekend?" Sioux hummed against her ear.

"I hate television interviews. Jane should know better. The last one I did is still being talked about." She groaned.

"Anybody can get the hiccups."

171

"See? Even you know about it and you didn't even work here." She moaned, recalling the burplike noises magnified by the microphone. "It was awful."

"That wouldn't happen again," he reassured her. "I'd be there with a glass of water."

"Last time the producer cut the interview for a commercial and scared them away by making ghoulish threats. I was the laughingstock around here for weeks."

"You'll be the calm, poised, beautiful woman I met the first day and fell in love with," he countered, kissing the tip of her nose.

"Promise I won't behave like a fool?"

"I promise to sweep you up in my arms and carry you away at the hint of the first hiccup. The audience will love it. Mad scientist kidnaps glamor lady," he teased in an attempt to make her smile.

This was no laughing matter. The wide yellow streak running down her back when she simply turned on a television wasn't the least bit funny. She'd do it for Jane and for Sioux, but she had strong misgivings about the outcome.

CHAPTER TEN

In the hushed hours before dawn Alexandria began trembling. Ten hours later, alone in a small boxlike room at the television station, she was certain she was registering an eight on the Richter scale. Sioux and Jane had both assured her the green tailored suit she was wearing was covering her lacy slip and there was nothing from lunch hanging from between her teeth, but deep in her bone marrow she knew catastrophe was around the corner. To avoid the possibility of hiccuping her way through the interview she had nervously gulped down a week's ration of water, which her kidneys had been faithfully processing throughout the day.

She could almost hear her sweat glands shouting, "Send more water!" And she did. Nervously wiping her hands with a white handkerchief Sioux had lent her, she prayed the triple dose of deodorant she had rolled beneath her arms wouldn't fail her. Mentally she imagined the poised male host of the late-afternoon talk show taking a deep whiff and passing out in front of the cameras. Doing this show was a living nightmare.

"You look great," Jane enthused as she breezed into the room and patted her on the shoulder. "A professional model couldn't look better."

Sioux's mossy-green eyes shone in appreciation as they reassured Alexandria that she was lovely.

"Sioux, is my makeup running?" she worriedly asked, touching her fingers to her cheeks to make certain it hadn't been washed off by perspiration. Alexandria was certain the makeup man had applied too much blush, and too much green eyeshadow, but when she had objected her protesting hands had been lightly slapped away with annoyance.

"Calm down, sweetheart," Sioux comforted her, dropping to his haunches, picking up her limp sweaty hand and kissing the back of it. "You're so nervous your finger is turning green beneath your engagement ring."

"Prewedding nerves?" she asked sotto voce to keep Jane from hearing. They had decided they were both too impatient to plan the huge folde-rol Alex knew Jane would insist upon. Instead, immediately after the interview, they were going to drive to the cabin and be married the next day by the minister of a small church in a nearby town.

Smiling broadly, Sioux winked. He turned her hand palm up and traced her love line with the tip of his tongue. The salty moisture exploded on his taste buds as he swallowed. "I could carry you out of here right now."

Perhaps rushing her to the altar hadn't been a good idea, but he couldn't take a chance that their loyalties would be divided again. While he had been reassuring Alexandria about the television show, they had been interrupted by Jane calling with plans about the wedding. Lady Jane expressed a desire to hostess a reception for five hundred at the country club. When they informed his mother of the upcoming wedding and the tentative plans, she stoically had not objected, but he knew she would feel out of place going from the production line to such a posh setting. Alexandria had enough reservations about marrying again without any further undue stress.

He loved her, wanted her to be his wife, wanted to shout it from the piney treetops. Those were the reasons he had rushed her out of the Beautiful Cosmetics building after they had made their announcement to Jane and his mother and had gone straight to the jewelry store to buy their rings. Over a champagne celebration dinner they made these private plans and followed them by going to his condo and making wild, passionate love.

Alexandria shook her head. "I guess it's like getting an allergy shot. For hours ahead of the doctor's appointment, I'd dread going. In the waiting room I'd work myself up to near hysteria. Then, inside the office, getting the shot, there would be a slight sting during the injection. And finally I'd leave the office hoping I'd never have to have another, but knowing I would."

"You are talking about the interview . . . not the wedding, aren't you?" Sioux teased knowing full well it was being in front of the camera that she dreaded.

For the first time all day Alexandria managed to laugh hoarsely. "I'm going to be calm tomorrow. Dead people don't sweat."

"You'll survive. I'm not about to let anything happen to you," he reassured her, chuckling at her macabre joke.

"It's time," they heard from the doorway. "Careful crossing the cables."

"Well," Alexandria said with a sigh as Sioux stood taking her hand and tucking it into the crook of his arm, "here goes nothing."

The stage was set with three comfortable chairs in a tight semicircle on a blue-carpeted platform. The skyline of Denver was portrayed in the background with the host's name blazing in the horizon as though it were the setting sun. A small table between the second and third chair held a pitcher of water and three glasses. Alexandria saw them and almost stumbled. Evidently Tom Schroeder had seen her last interview also.

"Break a leg," Jane murmured, wishing her good luck in the language of actors.

Sioux shushed Jane dramatically. Alexandria drily replied, "Thanks."

A clipboard filled with papers in his hands, Tom Schroeder advanced, a wide toothpaste grin on his too-beautiful-to-be-handsome face. "Well, Ms. Foster. We finally meet. You look fantastic," he complimented her. "Mr. Compton, would you sit on the outside? I like to keep the glamorous women close to me," he joked affably.

The three of them sat down in their assigned seating, a strained smile on the face of each of them.

"He's making shadow over her face," the crewman shouted from the darkness behind the bright overhead lights. "Move his chair slightly to the right and to the back of her," he curtly instructed.

Sioux didn't wait for the stage man to enter from the side; he made the adjustment himself. "How's that?" he shouted, reseating himself.

"Okay," the voice answered.

Alexandria had to turn her neck sharply and fluff her hair back off her shoulder to see him.

"Don't do that," Tom softly instructed. "Keep your eyes on me during the interview." Half-standing, he reached over and rearranged her hair. "Just relax; pretend you're at home in your living room, talking to friends."

Alexandria shot him a you've-got-to-be-kidding glare. *My knees are knocking in rhythm with my pounding heart; the heat from the overhead lights is making my head feel as though my brain is being baked; my stomach is doing solo try outs for the gymnastic events at the Olympics, and he tells me to relax?*

She glanced at the black-and-white monitor. It was the only way she could see the reassuring look on Sioux's face. Pasting a smile on her carefully glossed lips, she gathered her courage.

Sioux is here, she told herself. He loves me. He'll field any questions Tom thinks up to make the interview a sensation.

"Ten seconds. Look at *me*," Tom scolded when he saw her eyes glued to the monitor.

"Welcome to *The Tom Schroeder Show*," Tom greeted with his famous toothy smile when the camera zoomed in on him. "Tonight the subscribers of *The Rocky Mountain News* are going to meet two of their favorite people. Remember the front page picture of a woman and man embracing in front of the Beautiful Cosmetics building? Ms. Alexandria Foster and Mr. Sioux Compton," he introduced suavely, implying that the audience was about to learn the secret shared by the two guests.

The red eye pointed directly at Alexandria and Sioux.

Topaz eyes flashed in Tom's direction when Alexandria saw the newspaper picture superimposed behind them. She'd been the brunt of a TV host on a previous occasion. She knew his smooth-as-glass exterior hid the scalpel-sharp questions he was about to ask. Alexandria, literally, got a grip on herself by tucking one hand beneath the fullness of her emerald-green suit, and pressing her fingernails into the fleshy part of her palm.

"Did you interview Mr. Compton?" Tom prodded.

"Yes," she replied succinctly.

"And you didn't hire him?"

"Not at first," she admitted, glancing at the monitor and appealing to Sioux for a timely interruption.

"It's not uncommon to be interviewed several times before being hired," Alex heard from over her right shoulder. Sioux chuckled. His charisma was being picked up by the television camera and ultimately by the viewers. "I'd expected resistance, so . . ." His lips curved into a generous smile which made her heartbeat increase for a reason different from mere nervousness.

"So," Tom interrupted, drawing the focus of the camera back on himself, "you declared war on the cosmetics company whose slogan is: Beautiful Cosmetics, made for women by women."

Alexandria mentally swiped at the perspiration beading on her hairline. The heat was on . . . in more ways than one. It was her job subtly to defend their hiring policy.

"Qualified women," she interjected. "Mr. Compton's tactics were more . . . spectacular than those of other applicants, but he would have been hired once we realized he had a product American women have wished for but never dreamed could possibly be developed."

Alexandria breathed a sigh of relief. Tom had begun questioning Sioux about the product. Inwardly she smiled. Her ploy to distract the host from his original target had worked. For the first time she leaned back in the curve of the upholstered chair. Sioux was stringing out the discovery as though it were a mystery plot. Unable to turn and watch, she glanced occasionally at the monitor.

Tom was asking pointed questions, drilling

him with opaque blue eyes, but Sioux was dodging them, building the suspense. Slowly he withdrew from his pocket the before-and-after pictures of his mother. Leaning across the arm of her chair, he handed them to the interviewer.

"Can we get a close-up on these?" Tom asked.

Sioux pressed forward, giving Alexandria a reassuring smile. The broad smile drooped radically when he saw her face. Her makeup was turning a vivid red-orange. The places where the moisture had collected were a brighter orange than her cheeks. Only her eyeshadow was the original color: green.

"Oh, my God," he said with a groan, collapsing backward. He caught her smile in the monitor and realized she couldn't tell by the black-and-white picture what color her face was. Tom had been so intent on revealing the secret, he hadn't even glanced at her. "We're getting out of here," he said in a low, gravelly voice to the back of Alexandria's head.

"Shhhh. Not now. We have to plug the product," she whispered behind one hand in his direction.

Tom Schroeder glanced up from the picture, to Sioux, then to Alexandria. His mobile pretty face elongated as his chin dropped. Mouth twitching, he came close to a girlish giggle as he brought his face closer to hers. The cameraman was twittering also.

181

Sioux jumped to his feet, one arm dipped behind Alexandria's shoulders, the other under her knees. With what appeared to be a completely planned maneuver, he lifted her, turned his back to the camera, and kissed her as he exited the stage.

"What are you doing?" Alex hissed, pulling away from the pressure of his lips.

"You're going to be mad as hell," he gasped, making a closer inspection of her clown-colored face.

"Not going to be. AM! Jane will be livid." She struggled to get out of his arms and get back in front of the television audience. "Put me down. I'm going back in there."

"You're not," Sioux spat, clamping her swinging legs tighter and imprisoning her arms against his chest. He could hear laughter, bold, loud laughter coming from the stage site.

Sioux was tempted to carry her right out to his car and flee to the cabin, but he didn't want to embarrass her further by making a spectacle of her throughout the television station. Sighting a women's bathroom sign, he headed in that direction. Using his hip, he pushed against the door.

"You can't go in there," Alexandria shouted.

Sioux returned her to her feet and swiveled her bodily to face the mirror.

Alexandria's mouth dropped open and hung

loosely as she stared into the mirror. Had she been auditioning for a part in *The Wizard of Oz* she would have been appropriately made up. She batted her eyes, trying to right the wrong colors. "I'm orange!" She gasped. "I look like a damned pumpkin!"

"Must have been the heat from the lights combined with your being so damned nervous," Sioux said apologetically.

Alexandria could feel a scream building at the back of her throat. "The whole world saw my face, didn't they?"

What can I say or do? Sioux wondered. He couldn't deny the fact. Anyone who owned a color television set had seen the change of color and was probably fiddling with his color dial.

"I'm sorry," he whispered, desperately wishing he could think of something, anything, to obliterate the shock from her face. Grabbing several paper towels, he hastily ran water over them, then handed them to her dripping wet.

The damp coolness as she spread them over her face was a welcome relief. A hysterical bubble of laughter parted her lips and was muffled by the wet towels. "This is worse than hiccups," she laughed, her shoulders shaking.

"Don't cry. My God, don't cry. It was my fault. I'll explain everything. I'll correct the formula or resign."

Immediately Alexandria realized Sioux

thought her muffled laughter was sobs; her shaking shoulders caused by tears. *It's funny,* she thought, hysteria edging ever closer. *Here I thought the absolute worst thing I could do was have a siege of the hiccups.* Her head swam dizzily when she was turned and enfolded into Sioux's arms.

"Shhhhhh," he solaced her. "You're tearing my heart out. I wouldn't blame you if—"

Another burst of giggles was buried in the wet towels. His words were breaking through her hysterical thoughts. *He thinks I'm mad!*

"I'm not mad," she mumbled, her face held tight against the hard muscular wall of his chest. "It's hysterically funny."

The pacifying motion of his hand running from her shoulder blade to the small of her back abruptly stopped.

"Funny?" His grip loosened. His eyes sparkled when she stepped back, scrubbing her face, laughing the whole time. "But, but, but . . ." he stammered.

"You sound like a motorboat," Alexandria chided lightly. "Do I have the *miracle* product off my face?" she asked. Smiling, chuckling, she raised her orange-ringed face up for inspection.

"You aren't embarrassed? Upset?" Sioux asked in disbelief as he took the soggy paper and began swiping at the residue.

"Well . . ." She paused, honey-colored eyes

twinkling with merriment. "I do wish this had happened a month earlier. I know I should feel like a turkey, but I definitely look like a jack-o'-lantern. Wrong holiday!"

A deep rumble began in Sioux's chest—it sounded to Alexandria much like a volcano building up beneath a quiet surface—and erupted into loud guffaws moments later as it reverberated around the white-tiled walls. She saw the towels drop on the floor between them and felt herself being wildly pulled into his arms. Her feet left the floor and she was twirled round and round.

"I told you I trusted you implicitly. It never crossed my mind that you had purposely tried to make a fool of me," she reassured him.

The door opened and a wiry, gray-headed woman stuck her bespectacled face inside the crack. "Oh!" She gasped. "Excuse me. I must have the men's room. My dear, you'd better get out of here. Reputations are ruined for less!"

"My reputation is already ruined," Alexandria crowed.

"Alex! Alex!" they heard above a peal of giggles and masculine laughter. "Are you in there?"

The door opened again. Lady Jane stuck her head in, then entered. "This isn't a likely place for an executive meeting, but . . . thank God you didn't leave the building. I've been searching all over for you."

Feet back on the floor, Alex included Jane in the threesome hug. "How'd we do? We wowed them, didn't we?" she exclaimed exuberantly.

The worried expression on Jane's face switched to a smile. "A one-color base coat and you chose orange to be the color?" she teased Sioux.

"Look at it on the bright side. . . ." he began.

"My face was the bright side," Alexandria interrupted, lightly jabbing him in the ribs.

"Your face could have turned purple, or blue, or fuchsia!" he finished, punctuating each color with a sharp laugh.

"Or worse yet . . . wrinkled!" Jane completed. "Tom Schroeder was speechless for the first time in his career. They had to take a commercial break to cover his giggles."

"Suspicions confirmed," Alexandria hooted.

Nodding, Jane tried to keep a straight face as she reprimanded Sioux. "You know I should fire you, don't you?"

"Yes, ma'am," he answered, not really caring.

"But out of the kindness of my heart, I won't. Can't have my grandkids starving in the street, now, can I?"

Sioux and Alexandria smiled and winked at each other.

"Well"—Jane dramatically sighed—"I guess

you two better clear out of here and get up to the woods and get married."

"You know?" Alexandria squealed.

"Beautiful Cosmetics's grapevine knows everything," Jane answered mysteriously.

"You don't mind, do you?" Sioux asked, his voice filled with concern.

"Get out of here," Jane answered, pushing both of them toward the door. "I believe the coined phrase is: Be careful, and if not, name it after me!"

* * *

The journey to the cabin seemed only a mile away. Their combined melodic laughter put wings on the wheels of Sioux's car.

"Afraid of the dark?" Sioux whispered as he opened her car door and took her hand.

"Nope."

"Afraid of being alone in the cabin and waiting while I turn on the generator?"

"Nope."

"Aren't you afraid of the bears and creepy-crawlies?"

"Nope."

"What happened to the city girl?"

"Some savage Indian painted her with war paint to scare off the evil demons," she teased back. "Then he kept his promise and carried her off into the sunset to his teepee."

Sioux accepted her teasing and squeezed her shoulders.

"Ever made love out of doors?" he huskily inquired. His hand dipped down to the first button on her blouse.

"Never."

"Want to?"

"I'll get the blanket," she answered, breaking his hold and lightly tripping up the wooden steps.

Hand in hand, Sioux led and Alexandria followed as they headed toward the glade. The darkness of the pine forest enveloped them with its fragrance and its sounds, but none of them scared Alexandria. She knew Sioux's steps were sure and that he would not let her come to any harm. Trust, she mused. Blind trust. He'd earned it the hard way.

Lips tilted upward, she said softly, "We're in our own private world, aren't we?"

"My thoughts exactly." As they neared the glade the path became wider and Sioux draped his arm over Alexandria's shoulders. "A world we'll share regardless of where we are."

The moonlight filtered through the pine needles, casting silver peaks and shadowed valleys on his skin. "I love you, one," she admired softly as he spread the blanket on a bed of reddish needles.

"Why the 'one'?" Sioux knelt, pulling Alexandria down to her knees also.

"You're supposed to say, 'I love you, too,' " she whispered, lightly stroking the width and breadth of his wide shoulders.

"You're teasing when you should be serious . . . again," he softly chastised her. "I guess I'll have to learn to live with it."

Alexandria felt a mild shudder run from her knees to her head as he began slowly unbuttoning her blouse, tugging it from the waistband of her skirt.

"You should worry when I stop laughing. You'd have been in big trouble back at the television studio," she reminded him. Her own fingers copied his.

Moments later, as they lay unclothed on the blanket in each other's arms, Sioux gloried at the sweetness of her fragrance, the smooth silkiness of her skin, but most of all, the lit passion in her eyes.

"Want me?" he asked, his voice a mixture of gravelly desire and satiny love.

"Only on alternating days," she teased, knowing he knew she wanted him nightly, tricely.

189

LOOK FOR NEXT MONTH'S
CANDLELIGHT ECSTASY ROMANCES®:

All-new **Candlelight Newsletter**

An exceptional, *free* offer awaits readers of Dell's incomparable Candlelight Ecstasy and Supreme Romances.

Subscribe to our all-new CANDLELIGHT NEWSLETTER and you will receive—at absolutely no cost to you—exciting, exclusive information about today's finest romance novels and novelists. You'll be part of a select group to receive sneak previews of upcoming Candlelight Romances, well in advance of publication.

You'll also go behind the scenes to "meet" our Ecstasy and Supreme authors, learning firsthand where they get their ideas and how they made it to the top. News of author appearances and events will be detailed, as well. And contributions from the Candlelight editor will give you the inside scoop on how she makes her decisions about what to publish—and how *you* can try your hand at writing an Ecstasy or Supreme.

You'll find all this and more in Dell's CANDLELIGHT NEWSLETTER. And best of all, *it costs you nothing*. That's right! It's Dell's way of thanking our loyal Candlelight readers and of adding another dimension to your reading enjoyment.

Just fill out the coupon below, return it to us, and look forward to receiving the first of many CANDLELIGHT NEWSLETTERS—overflowing with the kind of excitement that only enhances our romances!